BOOKS BY QUINN AVERY
www.QuinnAvery.com

BEXLEY SQUIRES MYSTERY SERIES

The Dead Girl's Stilettos

The Million Dollar Collar

The Guard's Last Watch

The Skeleton Key's Secrets

The Notebook's Hidden Truths

The Neighbor's Dark Past

STANDALONE ROMANTIC SUSPENSE/THRILLERS

What They Never Said

In Her Father's Shadow

Woman Over the Edge

Deadly Paradise

Lost Girls of Kato

Moscow Mules & Murder

Right Across the Bay

CHILDREN'S BOOKS WRITTEN BY QUINN

Dogs Don't Have Fins

Dogs Don't Have Antlers

The Dead Girl's Stilettos
The Million Dollar Collar
The Guard's Last Watch
The Skeleton Key's Secrets
The Notebook's Hidden Truths
The Neighbor's Dark Past

THE NOTEBOOK'S HIDDEN TRUTHS

A BEXLEY SQUIRES MYSTERY

QUINN AVERY

PROLOGUE

PAPAYA SPRINGS, CALIFORNIA

MAY 18TH

Sylvia Renner's heart slipped into her throat as she darted around their $45M beach home overlooking the ocean, desperate to find her laptop. She was going to be late for the most important meeting of her career—one that could potentially earn her a hefty raise, and finally award her bragging rights as the family's main provider. Her husband Dennis had boasted about being the reason they were able to live a lavish lifestyle ever since they'd met twenty years prior, and she couldn't stand to listen to him one minute longer. Either she would earn a promotion as head publicist, or she'd divorce Dennis the moment their youngest left the nest. In her mind, there was no middle ground.

"Mom!" Reese shouted, her voice impatient and bouncing off the high ceilings. *"I need a ride to school!"*

"Where's your brother?" Sylvia called back, digging behind the deep sofa cushions in the theatre room. She'd agreed to watch a movie with her son the night before—a thriller with far too much gore and violence for her taste—and had fallen asleep halfway in. She swore she'd still been working on a movie pitch for one of her clients at the time, laptop perched on her stomach. So where was the damn thing?

"I don't know," Reese answered, her voice becoming nearer, "but his car's gone!"

Sylvia stood, her back tense with irritation. She didn't have time for whatever teenage drama had arisen between her children, resulting in Teddy leaving his sister behind. "Take the Beamer! I'm late for work."

Her youngest suddenly stood beside her, hands planted on her slender hips. Reese was a carbon copy of Sylvia at that age—fierce cheekbones, bright cornflower blue eyes, silky long hair the perfect shade of platinum, and a flawless body made for modeling. Sylvia couldn't imagine Reese's cropped tank top showcasing her bellybutton, and her hole-covered jeans skirt several inches too short for comfort would abide by the school's dress code, but Sylvia was beyond caring. It was the last week of school before summer break. What would they do? Send Reese home?

"You're joking, right?" Reese giggled, eyes hard. *"Mom.* In case you forgot, I don't have *my license."*

Sylvia's teeth clenched together. If she had used that tone of voice with her mother when she'd been that age…

"Then don't go over the speed limit," she told her daughter. "Obey the stoplights. Use your signal. It's only ten miles, Ree. You'll be fine. Most kids your age already have their license."

Reese let out a disgusted huff and spun around, trudging from the room. For a fleeting moment, Sylvia wished her daughter had been the one graduating, and not her angelic son. Teddy was an honors student who spent a lot of time at home as he didn't have many friends. Sylvia suspected it was largely due to the fact that none of his classmates were on the same level of intelligence. He did as he was told, and didn't talk back to his parents. *Ever.*

Meanwhile, there were days she was convinced

her sixteen-year-old daughter could benefit from an exorcism.

After Sylvia had upturned every cushion in the theatre, she slumped into one of the plush seats. She would have to resort to winging the meeting, and pretend she recalled every detail of the dating television show being pitched to the company's number one client. Temperance Rose was already a household name, thanks to her sweet nature that shone in the reality show that had made her famous. The multimillionaire's fans were rooting for Temperance to find true love after her heart had been demolished by famed actor-turned-serial-killer, Dean Halliwell. The new series had all the elements needed to become a world-wide sensation.

As Sylvia marched from the room, estimating how fast she'd have to drive in order to make it in time for the meeting, her phone buzzed from the pocket of her slacks. She didn't recognize the number, but it came from the Papaya Springs area code.

"Sylvia Renner," she answered briskly.

"Mrs. Renner, this is Deputy Adam Danks from the Currie County Sheriff's Office," a man answered in a soft voice with a faint Southern accent. "I'm afraid I'm calling with some upsetting news."

Sylvia's heart thrummed in her chest. Had something happened to Dennis? The man didn't exercise and was the prime age for a heart attack. "What is it?" she asked, grasping her cell phone tighter.

"Your son Theodore was involved in a serious accident."

Her hand shot out to brace the wall, holding her upright. "Oh God," she whispered. "Is he…"

"He's alive, but in critical condition. He was hit head-on by an elderly woman going the wrong direction down the highway. He's at the PS Hospital, being prepped for surgery. The ER staff will be able to fill you in on the details once you arrive."

A deafening whoosh swept through Sylvia's ears.

The man must've been mistaken. It couldn't have been Teddy. As a senior, it was his last day of school. They weren't required to take finals like the underclassmen. The night before, he'd been so excited about starting the rest of his life at one of the top universities in the country. He would be turning eighteen in just two days.

Not her baby boy.

The deputy cleared his throat. "Can someone give you a ride to the hospital, Mrs. Renner? I don't think it'd be a good idea for you to drive, all things considered."

"My husband will come get me," she muttered.

"I hate to relay this information over the phone," the deputy told her, "but there's something else you need to know. After they extracted your son from the car, one of the firemen spotted something disturbing—the item appeared to have been in the trunk at the time of the accident."

"What was it?" Sylvia demanded, her mind racing. Had they found alcohol? *Drugs?*

"Do you or your husband own any firearms?"

Her breath caught. "You mean *guns*? Of course not. Dennis and I both *abhor* any type of violence."

A long, deep breath rushed through her phone's earpiece. "You son was in possession of an unregistered handgun."

"You must be mistaken." Her hand began to tremble. Moisture burned the corners of her eyes. "Are you sure it was *his* car? Are you sure it was even *my Teddy*?"

"We'll discuss the matter at a later time, Mrs.

Renner." The deputy's voice softened. "For now, you and your husband need to be with your son."

Her cell phone fell from her hand, dropping to the hardwood floor with a loud clatter.

Sylvia stumbled through the hallways in a drunkard's walk. There had to be a misunderstanding. Her Teddy was a sweet, quiet boy, who had scored exceptionally well on his SAT. He was the furthest thing from a thug. He couldn't even stand to play violent video games. What reason could he possibly have to carry a gun? How would he have acquired it?

Moments later, she found herself in the center of Teddy's room. She was unaware of what she was looking for as she began rifling through his things. His desk. His dresser drawers. His closet. There was nothing out of the ordinary hidden anywhere—no drugs, no hidden video games, no pornographic magazines. Nothing to indicate he was anything other than a brilliant teenage boy with strong morals and a promising future.

Tears began to spill down Sylvia's cheeks. She flung herself onto her son's perfectly made bed, staring through blurred vision at the tongue-and-groove walnut ceiling. Maybe if she closed her eyes, she could drift asleep and wake to discover it had all been a bad nightmare.

But her gaze caught on the wall of shelves that stored his vast collection of classic novels and vinyl records. One item looked out of place: a spiral notebook.

PART I

CHAPTER ONE

PAPAYA SPRINGS, CALIFORNIA

MAY 19TH

The usual sensation of unease took flight in Bexley Squires's stomach as she perched in front of the camera, hands folded in her lap. She tapped her heels against the industrial carpet, eager to see the handsome face of the man she loved. Although it had been four months since Brewer Hawkins had been incarcerated, she still felt on edge at each and every visit she made to the Papaya Springs Jail. Something about the coolness of the artificial air, the stifling silence of the room, and the sharp antiseptic smell left her uneasy for hours afterwards.

Maybe it was simply because she dissected their

conversations afterwards, trying to decide if Brewer had been hiding something. She knew he'd die before he'd expose any weaknesses with a supervising jailer absorbing every word that fell from his lips. Brewer was an honorable man who had served his country. He'd also turned himself in after being coerced into acting as a drug mule for some of Papaya Springs's most influential leaders.

Bexley appreciated being able to hear Brewer's voice and look into his eyes as much as she despised seeing him out of his element. She'd never admit it to anyone, especially not to Brewer, but she had developed a routine after their late Friday afternoon visits. After showering under the hottest water she could stand, she'd slip into one of Brewer's t-shirts. His scent had faded from the soft cotton mere days after he'd left, but she remembered the way he'd look at her when she wore his shirt, and she'd tell herself it wouldn't be long before their lives would return to normal.

Either she was early for her visit that afternoon, or Brewer was running late. She covertly slipped her phone from her handbag to check the time, discovering a handful of missed calls and several texts from a phone number with a 507 area code. The last text from the unknown contact read:

. . .

CALL THIS NUMBER BACK A-S-A-P
  Extremly ergint

BEXLEY HAD TO READ THE MISSPELLED WORDS TWICE to be sure she understood their meaning.

"No cell phone use allowed in the visitor's area, *Squires*," a female jailer barked from behind her. "I'd think someone as *smart* as you could remember that by now."

Since Bexley had returned to Papaya Springs to work as a private investigator, solving crimes that *should've* been handled by the incompetent local law enforcement agencies, her list of allies with the men and women in blue was running shorter than ever before. She bit back a smart reply and stood to face the burly woman.

"I was just heading outside to make a quick call," Bexley told her in an artificially bright tone. "Would you be so kind as to let Brewer know I'll be right back?"

The tall, copper-tinted brunette hooked her thumbs inside her utility belt and grunted, pivoting her thick neck to the other side.

Bexley slipped into the quiet hallway where other visitors were waiting their turn. A few of them regarded her with curious glances. Most didn't bother acknowledging her. When she ducked out to the nearest exit, the chill she'd felt inside was instantly erased by the warmth of the California sun. She tapped on the 507 number in her call log.

After one ring, a breathy woman answered, "This Bexley Squires?"

"Yes it is. Who's this?" she asked.

"My name's—you know what? It don't matter." The woman's voice was deep and scratchy either with age, or heavy tobacco use. "I'm here with my neighbor's kid. She says 'er momma up and left two days ago, and she hasn't been able to get ahold of 'er since."

Bexley had tracked down many people as a private investigator, but none of them—that she knew of anyway—had involved an abandoned child. She immediately felt empathy for the girl. "Are you asking me to try to locate her mother?"

"No. I want you to come *get* 'er. I ain't runnin' no daycare."

But I am? Bexley mused to herself. "I'm sorry, ma'am, but my services don't include—"

"Not callin' for your services, lady." The woman

let out a dry, barking laugh. "I'm callin' 'cause she don't have anywhere else to go."

Bexley didn't understand. Had the woman drunk-dialed her? "How did you get this number?"

"The little girl found it. Said 'er momma had scribbled it down on an old envelope, and stuck it under a magnet on their fridge."

"And who is this girl's mother?"

"Sadie Roberts. Olive says she's your niece."

All at once the sun's rays became tiny laser beams, and sweat pricked Bexley's forehead. She had only recently learned of Sadie's existence, a half-sister allegedly conceived during one of her father's many affairs. Bexley hadn't mustered the courage to ask her father before his untimely death if there had been a DNA test, or if he'd merely taken Sadie for her word. Once Bexley discovered he'd sent thousands of dollars to Sadie, everything about the situation felt off.

No one had ever mentioned Sadie had a daughter. More importantly, Bexley hadn't the slightest idea that she might possibly be an aunt.

"Whether or not that's true," Bexley told the woman, "I barely know Sadie, and I've never met this daughter. Isn't there anyone else she can stay with? A grandparent? Family friend? Anyone she already knows?"

The woman let out another dry laugh. "The only nanna she knows is a ragin' drunk. I once seen her fist-fight Sadie in the yard. Besides, she moved down South years ago."

The start of a headache throbbed behind Bexley's eyes. "How old is this kid?"

"Nine…maybe ten. She's out back, playin' with my dog."

"Has Sadie left her like this before?"

"For a couple hours or two. Never overnight. Nuthin' like this."

"And this daughter doesn't have any idea where Sadie may have gone?"

"She don't have a clue. Said her momma ain't answerin' her phone, and her mailbox is full."

Bexley plopped down on the edge of the stone sign that read CURRIE COUNTY JAIL, and dropped her head into her free hand. "Have you called child services?"

"Listen, lady. Olive's a good kid. Maybe a little too chatty at times, but she's got decent manners despite who raised 'er, and she's real smart. If they put 'er in the system, Human Services will drag 'er through court and place 'er in different homes.

There's a real shortage of decent foster families around these parts. Some have done hard time for abuse. Who knows how she'll end up? At least with family, she's got a fightin' chance. Maybe you would only have to take 'er in for a few days. I can't get around too good—bad hips and everything. They bring me a meal every day, and there ain't enough for two of us. Olive only came over because she was outta food that wasn't rotten."

A massive wave of guilt crashed into Bexley. Brewer had been raised by an abusive foster family. He'd be disappointed if she didn't try to prevent this "Olive" kid from suffering the same kind of fate. She sighed. "Where are you calling from?"

"Blue Creek…Southwestern Minnesota."

Bexley had figured as much, considering that's where Sadie had been living at the time of her father's funeral. She let out a tired sigh. "I'm not saying yes or no at this point." She glanced down at her phone. The time she was allowed with Brewer was already cut down by five minutes. "You caught me right in the middle of something important. Can you give me a couple of hours to look into Sadie's whereabouts? I'll call you back to let you know if I've found anything. We'll go from there."

"Fine," the woman huffed. "I ain't goin' nowhere, and she's safe enough here with me."

Ending the call, Bexley rushed back inside. When she re-entered the visitor's room, her heart swelled. On the monitor, Brewer threw her one of his adorably dimpled smirks, chestnut eyes dancing with mischief.

He had packed on considerable muscle mass from bicep curls and push-ups. The jail's orange uniform stretched taut across his chest, and the sleeves looked dangerously close to cutting off the circulation on his inked biceps. Bexley was certain his intimidating size prevented other jailers from messing with him. Days after starting his sentence, he had shaved his thick brown hair down to an inch, and kept it short ever since. Although he also shaved his square jaw every morning, it was stubbled with a slight shadow by the time Bexley saw him. She imagined he'd sported a smilier look as a teenager in boot camp, long before he'd started building his extensive collection of tattoos.

The grown man sitting on the plastic chair on the video monitor was both fierce and handsome in a way that made it hard for her to draw in a steady breath. The day she'd get to feel those hulking arms around her couldn't come soon enough.

She responded with what was probably a child-ish, toothy grin. "Hey, you. Glad to see your skin still hasn't turned green."

His Adam's apple vibrated with a chuckle. "Maybe you should take a break from the Marvel movies, B. It wouldn't hurt you to watch a chick flick every once in a while." His grin grew. "Sure glad you could join me today."

Beneath the heat of his captivating gaze, she blushed. "Sorry 'bout that."

He lifted one thick eyebrow. "Is this the part where I have to remind you not to work yourself to death?"

"I'm not late because of work...I swear." She leaned in a little closer to the camera. "I just got the *weirdest* call."

"What could Bexley Squires possibly classify as weird?" he teased, mischief twinkling in his eyes.

"A woman in Minnesota who claims to be Sadie's neighbor said Sadie took off a couple of days ago without any explanation...leaving a ten-year-old *daughter* behind."

He shot her a dazed look. "Sadie has a daughter?"

"See? It's weird, right?"

"Yeah," he conceded. "This neighbor was hoping you'd know where to find Sadie?"

"She wants me to come get the daughter."

Brewer leaned back in his chair and ran a hand over his buzzed hair, eyes fixated on Bexley. "What'd you tell her?"

"I'll have to look into the woman's claims before I decide if I'm being hustled. Then maybe I'll talk to Cineste to see what she thinks."

"What if the woman is legit?"

"*Hawk*. I know more about what's under the hood of a car than I know what to do with a ten-year-old."

A deep, rolling laugh burst from Brewer's lips. "Give yourself some credit. You can't solve all of Papaya Springs' problems *and* know what a spark plug looks like."

The jailer muffled a laugh behind Bexley.

Embarrassment warmed her cheeks. Had Brewer's friends relayed every single conversation she'd had with them while he was away? "Colt told you about that?"

"He's not only running my shop while I'm in here, B. He's my eyes and ears to the outside world." Brewer's beautiful grin fell away. "No one else can take the kid?"

"Not without calling child services."

He reacted with a flinch that was too minuscule for anyone other than Bexley to detect. By that point in their relationship, she was able to read his mannerisms better than any book. "I know what you're thinking," she told him, her voice lowered. "I'm probably still a better option than the alternative."

"It's a tough call." He scrubbed a hand over the short stubble on his jaw and let out a noisy breath. "You'd be bringing a total stranger into our home, and I met plenty of deviant kids that age when I was in the system."

Though it made her sad to think of him in foster care, her belly warmed with the mention of *their* home. She was still in awe that he had secretly purchased the cottage she'd admired from afar, and fixed it up before telling her.

"Cap wouldn't let anyone mess with me," she said, trying to make light of the conversation.

One of his dimpled smirks slid over his lips. "How is that fur ball? He must be growing fast—he looked massive in the last picture you sent. Did he take you for a run this morning?"

"Are you kidding? I have no other choice. He has boundless energy. I'm starting to suspect his last owner was a marathon junkie." She purposely left out the fact that Cap, the mutt Brewer had rescued to keep Bexley company, was also ill-mannered. He'd either chewed or urinated on everything she owned.

Brewer chuckled. "Sounds like my kind of dog. Can't wait to run with him."

Her smile dulled. There were so many things she was looking forward to once he got out that it made it hard to get excited about the mundane day-to-day stuff, like eating and working on cases. Without her little sister, Cineste, and her best friend, Kiersten, stopping by on unannounced visits, it's likely she wouldn't have bothered wearing pants.

"What are you gonna do about the girl, B?" Brewer asked, his voice tender.

"I'm going to see if Red can track Sadie down before I make any decisions." If her trusted tech guru couldn't find someone based on their credit card and travel activities, it was usually because they didn't want to be found. "Maybe I can take care of this without leaving California."

"Solid plan," he said, nodding thoughtfully. "And if Sadie can't be found?"

Bexley sat quiet for a moment as she considered his question. She wasn't willing to miss her visits with him for anything. With her demanding case-load, she didn't have the time to hang out in the Midwest and wait for Sadie to get her shit together either.

There was a fair chance Sadie's daughter would be on summer break soon if she wasn't already. Bexley could fly up to Minnesota, do a little digging around to try to figure out what Sadie might be up to, and return before the weekend was over.

She lifted her chin. "Then I guess I'll have an excuse to finally pick out a bed for our guest room."

Eyes sparkling with approval, Brewer winked. Twice. It was the code Bexley had suggested for "I love you" in a letter to him early on, as she didn't want the jailers and his fellow inmates thinking he was soft. She also worried saying the words aloud in their current situation would become too emotional, and she'd break down for all to see.

Brewer had added his own spin to the idea, saying a third time meant, "I'm also crazy about you." He threw her one more wink.

For the first time since they'd worked out the code, Bexley winked back not just twice, but three times. Brewer chuckled heartily.

"As much as I'd love to watch you two *lovebirds* bat your pretty eyes at each other a little longer," the female jailer announced in a sarcastic tone, "your time's up."

"Ugh," Bexley responded, standing and rubbing the eye she'd winked. "Damn contacts."

It only made Brewer laugh harder, knowing she had never worn contacts a day in her life. The sound of his deep laughter would get her through the weekend.

CHAPTER TWO

An hour and a half later, amidst the faint odor of fresh paint in Stronghold Investigations, Bexley's assistant handed her a birth certificate. "I was able to confirm your *maybe*-sister from the same mister gave birth to a healthy baby girl by the name of Olive Renee Roberts in the booming metropolis of Blue Creek, Minnesota, ten years ago this fifth of July." Red's emerald eyes threw Bexley a tentative look. "The father is officially recorded as *unknown*."

Bexley scanned the document. "Did you find any pictures of the kid?" Though Olive's appearance didn't matter, it was a nagging curiosity she'd felt since the neighbor's call.

"That'd be a negative. Sadie's Facebook profile

was locked down tight. She only has one picture of herself made visible to the public." Red handed over a stack of mug shots. "This is Sadie's mom." They were all of an older woman with honey-blond hair and a narrow face. The woman shared several other physical features with Sadie—namely, big brown eyes and a large rack. "She's the only other relative of Sadie's I could find. *Linda* Roberts moved to a small town in western Arizona five years ago, and lives in a trailer park with a man fifteen years her junior. She has a pretty lengthy record that includes petty charges like public intoxication, disorderly conduct, and public indecency. She attended AA meetings for a few years, but she's holding a can of beer in every one of her recent profile pictures. The last known cellular number I could find under Linda's name has been assigned to a new user."

"Were you able to locate Sadie?"

Red popped a wad of pink bubble gum between her ruby red lips, and passed Bexley a credit card statement. "She's gone *way* off the grid. She hasn't owned a vehicle for several years, and the last transaction I could trace from her credit card is from Tuesday morning. She purchased a cappuccino from a convenience store only a couple of blocks from where she lives. If you want my guess, she's either hiding from someone, or she went along with someone who can take care of her. The only solid thing I was able to retrieve was her cell number."

Absentmindedly scanning over the bank charges, Bexley nodded. Even though Red was a wizard with technology, she couldn't find something that didn't exist. Wherever Sadie had gone, she wasn't using her credit card. For the first time since Bexley had received the call from the neighbor, she wondered if something might've happened *to* Sadie.

Red handed her another stack of papers. The top page included a candid of a severely wrinkled woman smiling with a mouth full of dentures and a white halo of hair surrounding her round face. "As for that wireless number you asked about, it belongs to a woman named Deanne Duncan, age seventy-three, retired factory worker. She's considered disabled by the State of Minnesota, and home health services pays her a visit three times weekly. They also bring her daily meals. Never married, no kids, and has lived in the same residence since she was forty-eight. She does in fact live in the house right next door to Sadie's last known address."

"Thanks for sharing your magician skills this late on a Friday night, Red. I'll try not to bother you for the rest of the weekend unless there's something important I need while I'm in Minnesota."

"It's no problem, boss lady. I'm kind of digging the whacky hours by now. You always know how to keep me on my toes." With a little shrug, Red twirled the tail end of her box-red ponytail around her fingers. "Besides…it's not like I had plans."

Bexley tilted her head, remembering the way Red had gushed for hours about the cute IT guy she'd met at some nerd-fest convention a month earlier. "No hot date with Jerome?"

Red's emerald eyes rolled toward the ceiling. "Jerome's history. Anyone suited to be my future husband would certainly *not* refer to Star Wars as the 'lamest soap opera in the galaxy'."

"Definitely not the guy for you," Bexley agreed. It was hard for anyone to miss Red's dedication to the franchise, considering the tattooed sleeve of Wookiees and robots that covered her arm, and the way she constantly quoted the movies in regular conversations. "He sounds… lame."

"That's the biggest understatement since the Battle of Yavin." Red grabbed her purse from beneath the front desk. With the palm of one hand extended over her head in her signature backwards wave, she pushed through the front door. "Safe travels to the Midwest!"

Bexley watched her leave with a smirk, grateful the quirky redhead had agreed to work under her employ. Even with the recent facelift Stronghold Investigations had undergone, replacing the paneled walls with drywall and adding a modern flare of streamline furniture, the office was still lacking in personality after her friend and mentor J.J. Stronghold had retired.

Bexley retreated to J.J.'s updated office, eyeing the patriotic wall hangings left behind when he'd turned the business over. Sitting in his worn leather chair brought up fond memories of all the times she'd gone to him for advice after he'd first offered her the job. She'd been hesitant to move into his office, afraid he'd think it had been easy for her to take his place, but something about the energy of the room allowed her to draw from his strength. Her father's sudden death had taught her she needed to carve more time out for the people she cared about, and she hadn't been good about staying in touch with J.J. after his COPD diagnosis.

She was still a year and a half away from completing the billable time required before she could apply for her own PI license, and she had so much to learn from J.J.'s decades of experience. Maybe once she returned—with or without Sadie's daughter—she could pay J.J. a visit, and finally take him up on the boat ride he'd offered on their last visit.

Bexley tried Sadie's number before she made arrangements for Olive to spend the night with the elderly neighbor, even paying for pizza to be delivered so they wouldn't have to share the woman's home-delivered meals. Then she booked a rental car along with an early, one-way flight to Minnesota. With the 2+ hour drive from the airport and change in time zones, she'd still arrive in Blue Creek, population 4,300, before lunchtime. She hoped she'd wrap things up early enough to bring the girl back to California on a late evening flight, but she supposed that was wishful thinking.

The reality that she would soon be acting as temporary guardian for a child she had never met on behalf of a woman she didn't fully trust weaved in and out of Bexley's conscience. What if the girl hated Bexley, and refused to leave? Olive could decide to pitch a fit at the airport, claiming she was being taken against her will. And didn't 10-year-olds go to bed early? Worse case scenario, Bexley could crash on Sadie's sofa for the night, and they could catch a flight the next day. Best case scenario, Sadie would show up to care for her daughter, and Bexley would be free to leave whenever she wanted.

She sent a text to the mobile media device Brewer had been issued as a well-behaved inmate.

HEADED TO MN IN THE MORNING. PLAN TO RETURN in time for our Monday morning date, so wear something nice.

SHE TRIED NOT TO SEND HIM TOO MANY MESSAGES as each one took a small chunk out of his monthly commissary. But there were times when she yearned for the assurance of his reply or words of wisdom, and the situation with Sadie's daughter was disquieting.

His one-line replies immediately started dinging on her phone.

BE CAREFUL, B.
You know very little about Sadie
She could be mixed up in something ugly
Let me know when you get there

> *Take it easy on the kid*
> *XO*

THE "XO" AT THE END OF HIS MESSAGES HAD MADE her scoff the first time he'd signed off with it, but she eventually began to appreciate how much the sentiment meant coming from a former "bad boy" who gave up younger women, cigarettes, and a motorcycle as his sole means of transportation—all because of Bexley's influences.

She was getting ready to call Cineste when she heard voices in the lobby. Part of her wished she had locked the door behind Red, but a wiser side of her acknowledged the biggest paychecks tended to materialize after-hours. When a well-dressed couple in their late forties appeared in the doorway of her office, she decided this visit was no exception. Collectively, the couple looked both exhausted and petrified. Their appearance created an odd sensation that trickled down Bexley's back.

The tall, slender man with red-tinted hair and a shock of freckles furrowed his graying brow, eyes bouncing between Bexley and the new placard on her door. Although he wore a trendy dress shirt and slacks, they were severely wrinkled as if he'd been wearing them for days. *"You're* Bexley Squires?"

Bexley warned herself not to bristle. Why did ninety percent of her clientele utter her name as if amazed someone her age/gender/stature/enter-other-asinine-reasons-here could solve anything beyond a third grader's comprehension? Would they be more accepting of her role if she bobbed her hair at her shoulders, and dyed it Nancy Drew blond?

Both Red and Brewer had chided her for greeting potential clients with heavy sarcasm. Apparently things like, "weird, that's the name on my driver's license too," and "why would they put *that* name on my door?" were unacceptable answers.

Metaphorically holding her tongue, she stood and nodded. "That's me. How can I help you?"

The woman's amber colored eyes were shadowed with anxiety and a soul-wrenching worry. Bexley knew the look as she'd seen it reflected in the mirror for months after Brewer left. Aside from that, the woman was a knock-out beauty. Brilliant sapphire eyes framed by long lashes brushed over her sharp cheekbones, and thick platinum hair slightly curled at the ends. Her floral dress clung to her curvy frame in a color that perfectly matched the vibrant tone of her eyes. The sparkle of valuable jewelry flashed from her wrists and earlobes.

"We didn't know where else to go," the woman said hesitantly, clutching a ratty notebook to her chest. "Temperance Rose told me you could... help us."

Once again, Bexley was reminded how lucky she'd been to befriend the influential reality star. It was the second time Temperance had sent someone to Stronghold Investigations.

Sensing the couple was deeply traumatized over something, Bexley rounded her desk and gestured to the two open seats. "Come on in and have a seat," she suggested in a gentle tone. "I'll see what I can do."

The woman moved slowly, as if her bones were brittle and she was twice as old as she appeared. As the man pulled a chair out for her, several carats worth of diamonds wrapped around his wedding band flashed in the fluorescent lighting. An uneasy feeling climbed up Bexley's throat as she sat across from them, waiting. She found herself wishing she'd taken a course in sensitivity while attending NYU.

"Our seventeen-year-old son was involved in a car accident yesterday," the man began in a grave tone. His hazel gaze didn't quite meet Bexley's. "The doctors did everything they can, but…we're not sure he's going to pull through. He's in a coma."

The woman whimpered into her clenched fist.

Bexley's stomach surged. "I'm so sorry, Mr. and Mrs…"

"Renner," the man answered. "Dennis and Sylvia." His tongue darted out, snagging against his paper-dry lips. "There's more to the story. But first we…uh…need your assurance that the information we're about to give you won't go beyond this room."

Bexley dipped her chin. "Of course."

"When they pulled Teddy out of his car, they found…an automatic pistol." Before he continued, Dennis wrapped his hand around his wife's. "According to the officer I spoke with, it's the type that shoots hundreds of rounds per minute."

"Any idea where it came from?" Bexley asked.

Dennis shook his head. "They said the serial number had been filed down." He lifted a quivering hand to rub at his brow. "We first assumed it belonged to someone else. It seemed more likely he had given a buddy a ride, and they placed the gun in his trunk without his knowledge." The man looked defeated as his free hand fell back at his side.

"You have to understand, Miss Squires, our Teddy is the senior class valedictorian at Papaya Springs Academy. He's not only highly intelligent, but kind. Quiet. We've never had any behavioral issues with him, including any degree of anger management. He's never even *held* a gun that we know of."

With a sickening sensation, Bexley suspected she knew the dark turn the conversation was about to take. "What was your son's destination at the time of the accident?"

"The high school," Dennis murmured. "And… there's more." He briefly glanced at his distraught wife. "Show her, Syl."

As if being roused from a deep sleep, Sylvia's thick lashes slowly fluttered. "What? Oh…right." She looked down at the notebook in her hands, hesitant. "My Teddy…he's always been a sweet boy." Her lips slightly curled at the edges as she passed the notebook to Bexley with a trembling hand. "We found this in his room, but it doesn't mean it was his."

"It's *his handwriting*," Dennis disagreed in a choked voice.

The single-subject notebook was curled at the edges like someone had obsessively bent it over and over. The plain blue cover was free of the usual doodling teenagers were known to make while daydreaming. Swallowing the sudden lump in her throat, Bexley began to skim through the notebook.

It began with a series of handwritten quotations by various poets and musicians. The universal theme was centered around "bad people" and "making changes."

Each page after the quotes began with a single name scribbled on the top line, followed by what appeared to be a list of grievances written in various colors of ink and pencil. Even the handwriting varied, sometimes recorded with so much pressure that the writing utensil bit into the paper. Tendrils of fear gripped Bexley's spine as she perused them.

UMA TREMBLY

-laughed at a kid for wearing something she didn't deem fashionable

-caught cheating in AP English and wasn't reprimanded

-backed into someone's car in school parking lot and didn't report it

LEXIE SWENSON

-parked in handicap stall

-threw a random girl's designer purse in lunchroom garbage

-slept with best friend's boyfriend…twice

-purposely tripped rival during track meet and broke girl's ankle

THE LISTS CONTINUED ON FOR SEVERAL MORE PAGES, only mentioning girls' names and revolting accusations. The last entry in the notebook consisted of a hand drawn map of what must've been the high school. Each room was labeled by a class name, such as "AP English" and "Geometry."

AP English was circled in red marker.

The names of the girls on the previous pages were listed in different rooms.

Bexley's heart stopped. "Have you shown this to the police?" she asked, glancing between the husband and wife.

"We don't think he would've followed through with it," Dennis reasoned with a constant shake of his head. "Besides, the map could've merely been a way for him to remember which classrooms to avoid. He clearly wanted to distance himself from these girls and their heinous acts."

The lump in Bexley's throat grew a little bigger. "And the gun?"

Dennis reclined back in the chair, lips clamped together.

A heavy silence hung between them.

Then Sylvia leaned forward, hands splayed over the edge of the desk. "Please help us, Miss Squires," she begged with tears rushing down her cheeks. "We don't know where else to go. *Please* help us prove that our sweet son isn't capable of planning something so horrific."

CHAPTER THREE

The small community of Blue Creek, Minnesota largely consisted of middle and lower class housing. The only luxury homes were located in a new division near the K-12 school with recently poured roads and sidewalks. Aside from a liquor store, several locally owned cafes, two chain restaurants, three gas stations, a library, and a hospital, there wasn't much else inside the city limits beyond trade businesses. The town was framed by farmland with rows of freshly planted soil, a narrow river, a cemetery, and miles of oak trees. The temperature was much cooler than California, but the greenery was lush, and the air contained an earthy freshness.

While following the directions to Sadie's house, Bexley sipped on her third cup of coffee that morning. After her meeting with the Renners, she hadn't slept a wink in the five hours before she had to drop Cap off and check in for her flight. The girls' names among the hand-drawn map of the school had been permanently etched into her brain, making it impossible to focus on anything else.

She'd surprised herself by accepting their case on the spot. She wasn't sure if it was because she wanted Sylvia to be right, that her son wasn't capable of what the notebook was suggesting, or because Bexley didn't have the heart to turn the grieving parents away without helping them uncover more answers. Before sending them on their way, she let them know that she'd be out of state for the weekend, and wouldn't be able to start on their case until Monday. Sylvia had thanked Bexley with a bone-crushing hug.

"You have arrived at your destination," the robotic GPS narrator announced.

Bexley pulled in front of a dilapidated mint green bungalow with moss-covered shingles. For whatever reason Bexley's father had been sending Sadie money, it clearly wasn't spent on repairing the house's exterior. Shards of glass on the front window were held in place with packing tape. Tall patches of grass surrounding the square house were overrun by weeds, and chunks of broken concrete created a walkway to the front door.

Shifting into park, Bexley grabbed her phone to message Brewer.

I'M IN MN. SADIE'S HOUSE LOOKS AS BAD AS THE place my father last lived in.

SHE LET OUT A DISAPPOINTED SIGH, WISHING SHE could tell him all the details of the Renner case. She needed someone with a level head to pick apart the facts she knew so far, and help her see it from all possible angles. There was no question she'd be paying J.J. a visit once she returned.

After she killed the engine on the compact car, she approached the house. She hoped the neighbor wouldn't see her right away and the house would be unlocked, giving her time to snoop around without Olive. When she raised her hand to knock on the front door, it creaked open.

A young girl around five feet tall stood in the

doorway, fists pressed to her hip bones in a Wonder Woman pose, sweetheart lips pursed with a cartoonish scowl. She was all skin and bones, but not in a sickly way. It was more like her limbs were growing at a rate too fast for her body to keep up with fat and muscle. The hot pink t-shirt and cut off jean shorts she wore hung on her frame, several sizes too large. She had the same big brown eyes as Sadie's, right down to the skeptical look they produced. Her fine, golden blond hair dangled just above her waistline, appearing in need of a thorough brushing.

"Can I *help* you?" the girl demanded in a voice an octave or two deeper than Bexley had expected.

Bexley's lips spread with an amused smile. She liked the kid already. "Olive?"

"That depends." The girl's eyes narrowed. "You the lady taking me to California?"

"*That* depends on whether or not we can find your mom."

A slight smile twitched against the girl's lips. "Are you really my aunt?"

Bending down to the girl's eye-level, Bexley took a deep breath. She sensed the kid was wise for her age, and it wouldn't help to sugar coat the situation. "I think it's important you and I promise to be honest with each other, Olive. I don't know for sure whether or not your mom is my sister, but your mom seems to believe it's true." Bexley tried to peer past the girl. "Have you heard anything from her since last night?"

"Nope." The girl swung the door open all the way, eyes lowering to Bexley's short boots. "I figure she won't come back for me, so Deanne told me to go home and pack a bag. I packed my swimsuit too, just in case. I mean…I've never been to the ocean before."

Sadness squeezed Bexley's heart with the sight of an ancient gym bag near the girl's feet. How would it feel to know your mother had split without warning, and there was no one left to care that you were all alone?

With a cheerful smile, Bexley held out her hand. "I'm Bexley Squires."

The girl's tiny fingers were cold. "I'm Olive Roberts. But sounds like you already knew that."

Laughing, Bexley released the girl's hand. "Mind if I take a peek around inside, Olive? I don't know if Deanne told you, but sometimes my job involves finding missing people. I might see something that would give me a clue where we can find her."

Olive's eyes popped wide. "Are you *a cop*?"

"No. I'm a private investigator. People hire me to help them solve problems."

"Go ahead, I guess." Olive's hands dramatically flew up at her sides. "My mom doesn't like it when *I* dig through her things, but she's not here to yell at us."

Bexley followed the girl into the house, shutting the front door behind them. The entry room contained a single sofa covered in laundry baskets and unfolded clothing. It faced a large flat screen TV that easily could've been more valuable than the house. Part of the parquet floor had been torn up between the entry room and the kitchen. Pots and pans with bits of moldy food covered an almond colored stove in the kitchen, and the single sink was piled with dirty dishes. The house had an odd stench to it, like dirty cat liter mixed with dust and rotten meat.

Bexley was crippled with the sudden need to grab Olive and run. If she had been a mandated reporter, she would've been forced to call the police. The conditions of the home were not suitable for a child—probably not even for an adult.

"Where's your room?" Bexley asked, hoping her voice didn't reflect her concern.

"I share one with my mom," Olive said. She wrapped her little fingers around Bexley's wrist. "Come on, I'll show you."

The first door down the hallway opened to a small bathroom with lime green tile. The next room, painted a bright yellow, couldn't have been bigger than Brewer's jail cell. A small dresser and a double mattress on a box spring took up nearly every square inch. A small pool floatie with a single sheet and a pink stuffed horse resting on a pillow sat at the end of the bed on the floor.

"It's a little bigger than the place we stayed in with my mom's last boyfriend," Olive explained. "She told me she'd find a new boyfriend we could stay with soon."

There were dozens of questions Bexley wanted to ask the girl. Had they always lived like this? Had Olive ever slept in a real bed? Did they essentially live out of suitcases? How many boyfriends had Sadie gone through in Olive's lifetime? Were any of them decent? Did Olive still know how to get in touch with them? What were these boyfriends' places like? Did her mom have a job?

There would be time for questions later, and Bexley wanted to think them through carefully. She was starting to think Olive could've developed an illness from whatever odor clung to the house. Whether or not Sadie returned, Bexley wasn't going to let Olive spend another night in the house.

Choking down the sudden rush of tears burning her throat, Bexley turned to the girl and smiled. "Why don't you grab your bag and head back to Deanne's house for a little bit? I'll come join you when I'm done, and we can talk about what we're going to do next."

"Okay." With a carefree shrug, Olive spun around.

Taking a wary glance around the room, Bexley wished she had thought to bring gloves.

The belongings left behind were as puzzling as Sadie's disappearance. In the dresser, Bexley found a stack of medical scrubs and ID lanyards from various nursing homes with other women's names. Under the mattress, a notebook contained user-names and passwords that also used other women's names. A hallway closet was filled with designer handbags still possessing both price tags *and* security tags.

Bexley took pictures of everything. She was certain it proved Sadie was a thief running a handful of scams. More than ever before, Bexley believed Sadie was lying about being their father's daughter.

There wasn't a single phone number for anyone to be found anywhere in the house. Again, Bexley tried calling the number Red had dug up, only to be informed by an automated voice that the user's mailbox was full. Bexley sent several texts, hoping they'd go through. She let Sadie know she was worried, and would take good care of Olive until she returned. She purposely didn't mention anything about the possibility of returning Olive to Sadie's care. That would involve an entirely different conversation.

Before heading over to the neighbor's house, Bexley called every hospital within a hundred miles to see if Sadie, or a Jane Doe fitting her physical description, had been admitted. Then she pulled up the surrounding counties' websites to makes sure Sadie wasn't included on their jail rosters. As Red had already done the same searches, Bexley wasn't surprised when the results left her empty-handed. Still, Sadie could've gotten into some trouble during the night.

Once she'd given the home a thorough search, she headed to the neighbor's. Deanne Duncan was more friendly in person, and lived in a well-kept home. While Olive played with Deanne's Beagle outside, the two women discussed every available option. Deanne's status as a nosy neighbor proved to be helpful, considering she knew each and every one of Sadie's friends by name, and could attest that none of them were able to provide a safe environment for Olive.

Bexley finally called Cineste. The sisters brainstormed for a solid hour.

"You're probably certifiable for volunteering to become that girl's temporary guardian," Cineste told her. "But at the same time, I agree the other options sound pretty grim."

"My schedule doesn't really allow for this kind of thing," Bexley admitted. "What would I do with her when I'm working?"

"I can help you watch her whenever I have free time. I mean I *am* studying to do this kind of thing…help kids in her situation. It might be beneficial to experience her struggles firsthand." Cineste let out a breathy sigh. "Just bring her home, Bex. We'll figure out the next step once you're here."

Twenty-seven hours later, Olive napped beside Bexley on a flight bound for Papaya Springs. Having never been on an airplane before, the girl had clawed Bexley's arm when the wheels lifted off the runway, and turned ghostly white as the plane climbed higher. Up until then, she hadn't stopped asking questions about California.

"Is it always sunny and hot?"

"Are all your friends famous?"

"Do you have your own palm tree?"

Bexley had experienced several moments of panic while in line for airport security. Leaving the state with a child she had just met was technically kidnapping. But after Olive declared to the agent that she was going to California for the first time with her aunt, the woman smiled and wished her a safe trip before she waved the next passengers ahead.

Olive didn't wake until the plane had parked at the gate, and everyone around them stood to retrieve their bags from the overhead bins.

"Are we in Hollywood yet?" she asked in a groggy tone, wiping at her eyes.

Bexley laughed. "Not quite, but we're about to visit someone who has spent a lot of time there."

It was a short drive to Temperance's estate from

the airport. Olive's eyes bulged as they passed security and pulled up in front of the star's massive home. The girl appeared dumbstruck by the three-story monstrosity as she trailed behind Bexley to the backyard.

Bexley, on the other hand, was smiling to herself because of the changes that had taken place since she'd first visited Temperance. The fleet of luxury cars parked in the yard for all to see had recently been auctioned off at a charity event. On Bexley's last visit inside the mansion, the whimsical decor had been replaced with modern furniture and a warm color scheme.

When Cap came charging around the corner of the mansion beside Temperance's fluffy white dog Cinderella, Bexley was reminded how much Temperance herself had changed. Cinderella's famous collar encrusted with diamonds—a gift from Dean Halliwell—was long gone, replaced by a pink nylon collar. Temperance had sold the diamond collar and donated every last cent to the families of Dean's murder victims.

With a rush of affection, Bexley squatted to greet her spindly puppy. Cap's entire body wiggled as he whined and licked every exposed inch of his master's skin. He smelled like dog shampoo, and his fur was smoother than normal. It was the first time she'd left Cap for more than a day, and she was surprised how badly she'd missed his companionship.

At his side, Cinderella sniffed Olive's ankles before standing on her hind legs, begging to be pet. Giggling, Olive sunk her hands into the Samoyed's thick fur.

From behind a rose bush with a pruner in hand, Temperance waved excitedly as she started for them. Barefoot in plain capri leggings, a one-shouldered t-shirt, and a panama hat pulled down to her eyes, the Spanish beauty still portrayed the part of a famous superstar.

"No way," Olive whispered, turning to Bexley with a sharp inhale of breath. "You know *Temperance Rose?*"

"*Hola*, Miss Bexley!" Temperance sang as she reached them.

"Hey, Temp!" Bexley replied, standing to greet her friend with a quick hug. "Thanks again for taking Cap on such short notice. I hope he wasn't too bad of an influence on Cinderella."

Temperance pulled away, laughing. "On the contrary. He taught her not to be so lazy. They've been on the run ever since he arrived." Her eyes sparkled when she smiled down at Olive. "Who's your beautiful *amiga*?"

Bexley set her hand on Olive's shoulder. "This is Olive. She's going to be bunking with me and Cap for a while."

"It's a pleasure to meet you, Miss Olive," Temperance sang. With a giggle, she watched her dog nudge Olive's hand, begging for another scratch. "My *Cenicienta* really likes you. Do you have a dog?"

"My mom says we can't afford it." Olive batted her eyelashes and blushed. "But I've..ah…always wanted a dog. Maybe she'll let me get one some day. I mean…if I ever get to go back home."

Temperance's smile slipped a little when she met Bexley's gaze.

Bexley turned to Olive. "Why don't you run around with the dogs for a bit? It'll do you good to stretch your legs after the long flight."

Eyeing the intricate backyard, Olive beamed with a grin. "Okay!"

"She's lovely," Temperance commented as they watched Olive race off with the dogs. "I simply adore *niñas* that age…so full of hope and energy. How do you know Miss Olive?"

"It's a long story," Bexley admitted. "She was in

a bad place, so I'm keeping an eye on her until I can find her a better option. Sadly enough, I may have to stick her in a daycare while I'm working. I don't think that's how she envisioned spending her summer." She turned to face Temperance. "When I dropped Cap off with your staff yesterday, I didn't get the chance to thank you for sending Sylvia and Dennis Renner my way. I'm going to have to start paying you a commission."

Temperance waved her hand, scoffing. "Sylvia has been good to me. I knew you'd take good care of her. If there's anything I can do to help, just say the word. I imagine you'll be busy with their case, and I have too much time on my hands. They wanted me to find *un nuevo amor* on the TV, but I do not wish to find love at this time. I wish to do something *importante* for a change—something to make a difference."

They watched Olive perch at the edge of Temperance's pool and slip her feet in the water. The girl's face split with a wide smile when both dogs snuggled up to her on either side.

With a sharp gasp, Temperance grasped Bexley's arm. "*¡Aye Dios mío!* I know what I can do! Miss Olive could come stay here with me during the daytime…while you work! Cap too!"

Reluctantly, Bexley shook her head. It was a brilliant idea, but she already felt as if she owed Temperance a thousand and one favors. "I don't know—"

"*Por favor*, Miss Bexley." Temperance's face became brilliantly lit with a wide smile. "I must insist."

CHAPTER FOUR

Olive and Cap sat at the bow of the 20' saltwater fishing boat while Bexley and J.J. stood behind the helm console. Both girl and dog angled their face into the afternoon sunlight, sharing twinned expressions of glee as the vessel skimmed over the ocean's small swells.

Bexley had only been on a handful of boats in her lifetime, and nothing about those experiences had been enjoyable. She was surprised by how much she got a thrill from the tranquility of gliding across the water alongside her mentor. The warm air cleared her mind, and made her appreciate living in the moment rather than worrying about whatever turmoil was slated to come into her life next.

Even with a portable oxygen tank nearby, she'd never seen J.J. quite so happy or relaxed. His leathered skin had taken on a deep brown glow, and a constant grin was fixed on his lips. In khaki shorts and a red button down with a tropical floral print, snow-white hair, and mustache portraying a handsomely shaggy look, he reminded Bexley of an older *Magnum P.I.*—the investigator in the Captain's favorite tv show from the 80s.

"Looks like they're both enjoying themselves," J.J.'s deep voice rolled with amusement.

Bexley nodded. "Olive said she's never seen the ocean before. For all I know, Cap hasn't either."

"How's Brewer holdin' up?"

"He's…good. Still working out to pass the time. We're going to need a bigger cottage by the time he's released, just to fit his biceps."

J.J. chuckled with a smoker's rumble. "So what's this about a case you wanted to run by me?"

Her shoulders fell. "It's a real doozy. I'm not completely convinced I did the right thing by accepting it."

With his gaze set on the horizon, J.J. shrugged. "I'm sure you did, darlin'. You have a good sense for things."

Sometimes the man had *too much* faith in her,

Bexley thought with a slice of irritation. She turned away from him. "An affluent couple came to see me after their seventeen-year-old son was involved in a serious car accident on his way to school. Law enforcement discovered a semi-automatic pistol in his car, and the parents found a notebook in his room with a list of ill-advised acts committed by female classmates along with a hand-drawn map of the school with the girls' whereabouts." She forced out a short breath. "The parents want me to somehow prove their son wasn't the monster that the gun and notebook would suggest. I can't overlook the fact that he only had one gun in his possession when he's smart—the class valedictorian. If his intention was to harm more than one of his classmates, he would've needed an arsenal. But what other motivation could this kid have aside from a school massacre?"

J.J. was quiet for a moment as he pursed his lips, nodding. "You're questioning the morality of it all."

"Do I have an obligation to turn the notebook into the police?"

"You and I both know things aren't always what they seem to be on the surface. Get a sense of this kid...talk to his friends and teachers, the school principal. Interview the classmates on the list to see what kind of relationship—if any—they might've had."

"What about the notebook?"

"No sense in getting the police involved unless the boy recovers, and you find information that proves he'd planned something malicious."

She could already breathe a little easier knowing J.J. didn't blame her for taking the case.

The boat caught the inside of a swell, spraying saltwater over the hull. Olive squealed, and Cap barked before shaking the water from his coat. Laughing, Olive held her hands up.

J.J. smoothed his fingers over his mustache. "What you plannin' to do about the girl?"

"I have an address for Sadie's mother in Arizona, but no current phone. I might take a trip out to visit her, see if she's either fit to care for Olive, or knows where I can find Sadie."

"Maybe you can get the inside scoop on her relationship with your pops while you're there."

Unease wove through Bexley, clenching her stomach. She hadn't thought of confronting the woman about her relationship with the Captain. Could it really be that easy to finally learn the truth?

As she watched Olive sling an arm around Cap,

Bexley thought of the shocking condition of the house back in Minnesota. What would it mean for Olive if Sadie had lied about being the Captain's daughter?

EARLY MONDAY MORNING, OLIVE ROUSED FROM HER makeshift bed on the sofa with the aroma of the blueberry pancakes Bexley had prepared using muffin mix from a box. Bexley noted the girl must not've slept well by the way her wrinkled pajamas twisted around her little body, and her blond hair hung in knots. She sent a text to Cineste, asking if she'd help pick out a mattress and bedding for the unfinished guest room some time later in the week.

After dropping Olive and Cap at Temperance's, then stopping by the jail to fill Brewer in on her trip to the Midwest, Bexley convinced the academy's principal to carve time out of his "extremely busy" day to meet with her.

The Papaya Springs Academy campus sprawled over twelve blocks near downtown, and wasn't easy to navigate around. The private high school, able to accommodate a thousand students, was only a couple of years old and equipped with the latest technology. With an entire building dedicated to future IT careers, its sophisticated vibe rivaled some of the most advanced universities in the world. The wealthy residents of Papaya Springs wouldn't settle for anything less when it came to the education of their children.

Twenty minutes after she'd parked in the staff parking lot, Bexley was ushered into a pristine office with a glass wall that provided stunning views of the ocean. Principal Banks was slim and tall with authoritative eyes and short, dark hair featuring tufts of white. He'd been with the school for twenty years—five as a math teacher—and was set to retire the following year. From behind a desk piled with a mountain of paperwork, he folded his spindly hands and didn't even attempt to offer a friendly smile. Bexley sensed he had mentally checked out months ago.

"What can I help you with, Miss Squires?"

"I'm wondering what you can tell me about Teddy Renner."

"You're here because you're investigating his accident," he assumed, soothing the deep grooves in his forehead with his thumb and pointer finger. "It's always the ones you least expect," he muttered to himself, glancing down. "Damn kids." With a sneer, his eyes snapped back to Bexley. "Was he drunk? High?"

"Neither," Bexley answered. No one else would be privy to the unregistered firearm in Teddy's trunk as he had been only days short of his eighteenth birthday, and would be charged as a minor. "I'm *here* because I was hired by Teddy's parents to look into his state of mind at the time of the accident. They have reason to believe he was under a lot of duress."

Principal Banks relaxed a little, and shrugged. "Teddy's an exceptional student—one of the brightest to ever walk these hallways. He's always placed high expectations on himself."

"But I understand he wasn't expected to take finals because of his grades and the fact that he's a senior. At this point, his expectations shouldn't have been an issue. Are you aware of any other reasons he may have had to feel added pressure?"

"Nothing that I know of."

"What kind of relationship does he have with his classmates?"

The principal rubbed his chin thoughtfully. "He has one or two friends. Other than that, I don't think he's particularly liked by the other students. They tend to envy the most scholarly ones. They're under a lot of pressure from their families to be the best of the best."

"Can you give me the names of these friends?"

"Dalton Hulbert and P.J. Howard, although I don't believe I've seen Teddy with Dalton for some time. At least not since Dalton started dating Brooke Walters."

Bexley scribbled the boys' names with her stylus onto her phone's screen. They were the two names Teddy's parents had also provided. Beyond that, they didn't seem to know much about their son's social habits. "Have you heard rumors of Teddy dating anyone?"

"From what I've witnessed first hand? It's highly unlikely. He enjoys flirting with pretty girls, but they all seem to scoff at his advances."

"Do you know if he was ever a target of bullying?"

"We don't tolerate bullying at PS Academy," he replied sharply, eyes narrowing.

"What about the teachers? Did he get along with them?"

Leaning back on his chair, his tense posture eased into a shrug. "I believe he maintained an amicable relationship with a majority of them. There'd been a few complaints over the years that he was unteachable, and believed he knew every-thing. One teacher recently claimed that Teddy told him someone who can't make more than a 'lousy teacher's salary' shouldn't be teaching anyone above their own IQ."

Thinks he's smarter than his teachers, Bexley added to her notes. "Do you happen to remember which teacher that was?"

"Fred Finnegan."

Bexley nearly laughed aloud. "*Fred Finnegan* became a teacher?"

A number of memories from her high school days with Fred resurfaced—most of which were unpleasant. Fred and his brain-dead teammates shoving underclassmen into lockers, sexually harassing the popular girls, manipulating teachers into letting them cut class and basically do whatever they wanted. She could possibly envision him as a coach, but the overly confident jock she'd known had received a diploma despite a number of failing grades. Rumors that his parents had paid the school off ran rampant in the weeks leading up to their graduation.

"You're familiar with Fred?" the principal asked with a bright smile. "He's one of our most well-liked faculty members here at the academy. Teddy was in his AP English class."

Bexley's stomach churned. Teddy had circled "AP English" in red. "Is Fred on the campus today?"

"I believe so."

Bexley quickly stood, throwing her handbag over one shoulder. "I'm going to need directions to his classroom."

———

THE STRONG SCENT OF MEN'S AFTERSHAVE overwhelmed Bexley as she entered the main floor of Fred Finnegan's classroom. It was similar to a college lecture hall, with enough tiered seating for hundreds of students and a colossal smart board mounted over the lectern podium. Alongside a bank of windows that afforded a remarkable view of the ocean, Fred leaned back with one arm slung over a leather chair, heels of his crossed legs propped on a streamline black desk, devilish grin stretched over his lips while watching something on his laptop in front of him.

Back when Bexley had been a teenage girl ousted

for being unlike her classmates, she'd had a hard time seeing anything beyond Fred's cocky attitude. Now, she had to admit that he'd become undeniably attractive in the past decade. Strong muscle tone, sharp bone structure, tanned skin, a few days' worth of dark scruff shadowing his square jaw, lustrous brown hair and thick eyebrows over dark eyes—she'd even go as far as to say he was wildly handsome. In a white dress shirt rolled at the elbows, khaki shorts, and leather sandals, he could've still effortlessly fit in on a college campus.

"Sorry to interrupt," Bexley called out, "but I was wondering if I could have a few minutes of your time to discuss one of your students."

Eyes as wide as stoplights, Fred slammed his laptop closed and bolted to his feet. When he cleared his throat, his scowl fixed on Bexley was as hot as fire. "Next time you might wanna try knocking before barging into a classroom."

Caught with his hand in the proverbial cookie jar, Bexley mused. She didn't *want* to know what he'd been watching. "The door was open."

"I keep it open for *my students*. A few have stopped by to turn in late assignments." With a tilt of his head, the scowl began to fade. "Do I know you?"

She sure as hell hoped not. She wasn't about to remind him who she was in case he did. "I'm a private investigator, hired by Teddy Renner's parents. They have reason to believe he was dealing with some personal struggles at the time of his accident."

Fred's eyes rolled upward. "I won't have anything useful to tell you about *that* kid."

"Because the two of you don't exactly see eye-to-eye?"

"Who told you that?"

"Principal Banks. I just left his office."

Running his fingers through his thick hair, he glanced away. "He's a privileged brat who doesn't understand the concept of respecting his elders *or* working hard to earn a grade. That's the extent of what I know about him."

"Principal Banks claims he's an exceptional student."

"Maybe for his other teachers."

"What was his final grade in your class?"

"I gave him an A. I had no other choice—I was pressured from all sides."

"Pressured?"

"His parents are a powerful influence at the academy."

Bexley lifted one eyebrow. "Are you suggesting his parents paid his way through school?"

With a frown, Fred shrugged. "It happens."

"So I've heard." She pressed her lips together to prevent herself from saying anything more on the subject as she approached him. "Walk me through this beef between the two of you." Folding her arms over her stomach, she titled her head and leaned a hip against his desk. "How did it start? Was Teddy openly hostile towards you? Did he ever threaten you, or give you any sort of reason to fear him?"

"You mean other than the time he *claimed* I humiliated him?"

She nodded. "Sounds like a good place to start."

With a dramatic sigh, he plopped back down into his chair. "It came to my attention that Teddy was aggressively trying to score a date with one of the academy's most popular students—a girl he sat by in my AP class. It was ridiculous, really...he wouldn't have a chance in hell with her. One day I saw them engaged in a conversation, and she was grimacing. She clearly wanted to be left alone, so I called him out on it."

"In front of the entire class?"

A prideful smirk pressed against Fred's lips. "More or less."

Bexley decided he was still the same jerk he'd been in high school. "What was the girl's name?"

"Uma Trembly."

Bexley's heart thumped hard.

Uma was the first girl on Teddy's list.

CHAPTER FIVE

Red was unable to locate Uma Trembly's current residence, but she promptly provided addresses for the two friends of Teddy's named by his parents and Principal Banks. Bexley visited both posh mansions with million-dollar ocean views, not exactly surprised when no one answered the door. She also tried their last known cell phone numbers, directing them to return her call in voicemails. She hadn't expected the boys to be home mere days into summer, but most teenagers treated their cell phones like another appendage. She suspected there was a reason they were avoiding any requests to speak with a private investigator. It seemed she was going to have to get more creative in order to speak with them.

She returned to her office to pour over Teddy's notebook, waiting for something to stand out. Had the other girls on his list rejected his advances too? Did the friends know what Teddy had been planning? Had Teddy harassed Uma to the point that she'd become afraid of him?

After completing the mundane leg work on an insurance fraud claim and what must've been her hundredth infidelity case, she made several unproductive calls back to Minnesota in another attempt to locate Sadie. It made Bexley physically ill to think Sadie might actually be okay, and not at all interested in her daughter's wellbeing. She mapped out the route to Sadie's mom's last known address in Arizona. Once she made more progress on Teddy's case, she'd make a trip down to visit Linda Roberts.

By the time the end of her work day rolled around, the start of a headache along with a sense of failure pressed against her skull. The only thing she'd accomplished all day was uncovering a motive that would suggest Teddy had intended to carry out his parents' greatest fears. More than anything, she wanted to sit on the beach and nurse a bottle of wine. But responsibility called. She had to retrieve Olive and Cap, then figure out what to make for dinner.

When the spirited nine-year-old and two dogs came bounding toward her behind Temperance's mansion, Bexley stopped dead in her tracks. Not only were Olive's blond locks trimmed just past her shoulders and styled in a healthy, fashionably layered cut that highlighted her pretty face, but she wore a new pair of shorts and a beautiful yellow top with straps that showed off her golden shoulders. Even her ratty flip flops had been replaced with strappy white leather sandals.

As soon as Olive noticed Bexley's stunned expression, she stopped to take a dramatic pose and fluff her hair. "What do you think?"

"I'm here to pick up a girl named Olive," Bexley answered, bracing herself as Cap slammed into her legs. "Have you seen her around here anywhere?"

With a sudden light in her eyes, Olive giggled. "I really hope you're *joking*."

"*Hola*, Miss Bexley!" Temperance called out, heading toward them in a colorful sundress, dark hair styled in camera-ready waves that tumbled over one shoulder.

"I was just having a chat with one of your costars," Bexley teased, motioning to Olive.

Temperance stepped in behind Olive with a

bright smile. "You joke, but this one could truly be a star."

Bexley crouched down to scratch behind Cap's ear. "You didn't have to go to so much trouble."

"It was no trouble at all!" Temperance insisted, squeezing Olive's shoulder. "My stylists were excited when I asked them to come in to do a makeover. They're helplessly bored since I hardly go out anymore. They miss dressing me up like their doll."

"Well, it was sweet of you to do this for her," Bexley admitted. "What do you tell her, Olive?"

Olive spun around, clutching her thin arms around Temperance's waist. "Thank you, Miss Temperance! I had so much fun today!" Temperance's dog Cinderella barked and stood on her hind legs to join in on the embrace.

With a tinkling laugh, Temperance squeezed Olive back. "Me too, *bella*!" When Olive stepped back, Temperance bent to kiss the top of her head and whisper something into her ear.

Although slightly jealous of the bond they had already formed, Bexley was touched to see a more playful side of the hardened girl she'd first met in the dilapidated house in Minnesota. She wondered if Sadie had ever shown her daughter any degree of care, or if random boyfriends and criminal acts were a priority.

"Does it still work for them to come by the same time tomorrow?" she asked Temperance.

"Of course! They're always welcome in *mi casa*. If I ever have a scheduling conflict, I'll let you know ahead of time."

Olive threw an enthusiastic wave in Temperance's direction. "See you tomorrow!"

"*Adios, bella!*"

As they turned to leave, Bexley looked over her shoulder to mouth, *"thank you,"* with a sincere look. She didn't know how she'd ever repay her beautiful friend for her kindness. Temperance responded with a wink, then blew her a kiss.

As they loaded into her SUV, Olive asked, "When do I get to meet your boyfriend?"

The question took Bexley by surprise. She was sure she hadn't mentioned Brewer, although she supposed Olive could've seen evidence of him at the cottage. "How did you know about him?"

"Temperance told me. I asked her if she had a boyfriend and she said she didn't, but she hoped one day she could find one just like yours. She said he's dreamy and brave, and treats you like a queen."

As Bexley started the engine, she grinned through the windshield with a slight flush burning her cheeks. "She's not wrong."

"So when do I get to meet him? Temperance said you visited him today. Why isn't he at your house?"

While maneuvering out of the complicated driveway, Bexley carefully considered her answer. With Sadie's history, she suspected Olive was no stranger to the concept of jail, but she didn't want Olive to assume Brewer was a criminal when it couldn't be any further from the truth. "He had to…go away for a while."

Olive made a humming noise. "Sounds to me like he's in prison."

"Brewer's in jail, not prison, but he's actually one of the good guys," Bexley insisted. She swallowed the lump in her throat, doubting she'd ever be able to talk about his hardships without experiencing a strong surge of emotions. "He's fixing a mistake he once made during a hard time in his life."

"Temperance told me you stop bad guys for a living. Do you shoot them?"

Bexley briefly held Olive's curious gaze in the

rearview mirror. "That's not a part of my job description."

"Then how do you stop them?"

"Well, I try to prove someone is guilty of something, then I alert the police so they can arrest them." *If only it was actually that simple,* Bexley thought with a mental roll of her eyes. "In some cases, like one I'm working on now, I actually try to prove someone is *innocent.*"

"Why? Because you like them the way you like your boyfriend?"

"Because his parents hired me to prove he wasn't really planning to hurt anyone."

"Why don't you just ask him?"

"Because he was in a car accident, and now he's in a deep sleep."

Olive's big brown eyes popped wide. "You mean he's in a comma?"

"Coma," Bexley corrected.

"When will he wake up?"

"The doctors don't know."

"It would be nice if you could prove he wasn't planning to hurt anyone before he wakes up."

"I agree, Olive. It would be nice." Bexley resisted the urge to drop her head on the steering wheel. What if Teddy never regained consciousness? What if she wasn't able to prove to his parents that he was the good son they believed him to be?

On the remainder of the ride, Olive and Cap literally bounced off the backseats. With the sight of Cineste's blue Acura in her driveway, Bexley released a noisy sigh of relief. Being a pseudo parent was already proving to be a challenge. She was willing to take any help she could get.

When stepping through the front door, it was apparent by the pile of plastic wrapping and cardboard that Cineste had supplied everything needed in the spare bedroom. Not only that, but the heavenly aroma of pasta slammed into her with the force of a plane jumper without a parachute.

"Hello!" Cineste called out. She darted around the wall separating the kitchen from the entryway to greet them. Long brown hair pulled back into a neat ponytail, face glowing, pink floral apron secured over her shorts and T-shirt, Bexley's little sister looked the perfect part of a 50s housewife. Cineste crouched down to Olive's level, hands planted on her knees. "You must be Olive."

"That's right," Olive confirmed, jutting her chin with attitude. "Who're *you*?"

Flinching with the bold question, Cineste glanced in Bexley's direction. "Is she for real?"

Despite the laugh tickling against Bexley's throat, she threw Olive a scolding look. "The polite thing to do would be to offer your hand for her to shake and say, 'hello' before asking her name in a… uh…nicer way."

"That's okay," Cineste decided. She offered her slender hand to Olive. "I'm Cineste, Bexley's sister. It's nice to meet you."

"So you're my *other* aunt," Olive said, eyebrows raised.

As Bexley and Cineste exchanged an unsure look, Alex rushed through the door behind Bexley with Cap on his heels. "Does this guy have an off switch?"

"Temperance said he just needs a little training," Olive announced, bending to scratch behind the dog's ear while he lapped her face. "She says he has a big heart."

"It must be fun spending time with Temperance at her place," Cineste said.

"She let me try on her shoes, then a bunch of people came to give me a haircut and new clothes." Olive stood a little taller, beaming with pride. "She said now I know what it's like to be a movie star."

Cineste grinned. "I wouldn't mind spending a day or two there."

"Whatever you made smells amazing," Bexley told her sister. "How long until it's ready?"

"Just as soon as you put on something more comfortable than that blazer and those dress pants. Alex set up the table out back."

Bexley moved in to hug her sister, surprising them both. "Thanks, sis," she whispered into her ear. "I truly don't know what I would've done without you these past several months."

Cineste squeezed her back with a snort. "You would've been wandering around on the beach, butt naked, muttering incoherent nonsense." She spun around to face Alex. "Dinner is almost ready. You can take the parmesan and napkins out."

Eyes twinkling, Alex leaned on the countertop. "Can I first take a moment to appreciate the visual of your sister naked on the beach?"

Cineste squealed and grabbed the towel from the oven handle, snapping it at his backside. He scurried outside, chuckling as she chased after him.

"Your sister seems really mad that her boyfriend wants to see you naked," Olive commented.

"He was only teasing her, Olive."

"How do you know? My mom says when a guy talks about you that way, they want a lot more than your phone number."

Stopping to take a deep breath, Bexley answered, "Because he loves my sister, and he knows I love Brewer. Sometimes people who are in love like to push each other's buttons for fun."

With a dramatic snort, Olive rolled her eyes. "Adults are weird."

ONCE DISHES WERE DONE, CINESTE AND ALEX headed home. Bexley settled in the backyard with a freshly corked bottle of Prosecco, promising herself she wouldn't indulge in more than one glass while Olive threw sticks for Cap in the sand. As she savored every sip of the sparkling white wine, her mind began to wander…to how much she wished Brewer was there, how much she despised Sadie, what she was going to do with Olive, how she'd save Teddy, why her conversation with Fred bothered her when she gave it more thought…

Next thing she knew, she bolted awake with the sound of a musical female voice. "You must be that private investigator all of Papaya Springs has been going on about…Bexley Squires."

Bexley had to rub the sleep from her eyes before they'd focus on the short, graceful woman hovering over her. The slight wrinkles around the woman's eyes and neck, along with long silver hair braided away from her narrow face suggested she was in her late sixties to early seventies. Under one arm she held a blue vase filled with vibrant pink flowers. She donned so many bright colors in different fabrics and dangling jewelry that Bexley couldn't decide where to look first.

The woman snatched the wine glass from Bexley's lax grip. "You look as if you've had a long day, my dear. Maybe it's time for you to tuck yourself in for the night."

Remembering she had fallen asleep watching Olive and Cap play by the water, Bexley bolted from her chair and called out, "Olive? Cap?"

"The girl and dog are safe inside." Without the slightest hint of malice in her tone, the woman added, "Probably a good place for them, considering they teamed up to destroy my prized rock roses." She then handed the flowers to Bexley. "I figured I'd bring them over for you to enjoy, rather than let them go to waste."

Embarrassment swept over Bexley as she glanced down at the bouquet. "I'm truly sorry about your flowers, but you must be mistaken. I couldn't have been out for more than a few minutes, and those two couldn't have gone far, Ms…?" She paused, waiting for the woman to introduce herself.

"Finn. Twila Finn. I'm your next-door neighbor."

Bexley was beginning to suspect the woman was nuttier than a jar of Planters. "We…don't have neighbors, unless you live in the rocks." *Like some mythical creature,* she silently added. Maybe Bexley was dreaming the entire conversation.

"I live half a mile in the *other* direction. My place isn't easy to spot from the beach. I keep the lot overgrown as I rather enjoy the solitude." Folding her arms, Twila released a sly smile. "That is until my new neighbor's delinquent child and untrained canine came along."

Wincing, Bexley raised the palms of her hands. "*Please* don't call the police over this, Miss Finn. I'll replace your flowers—whatever you want. Olive is only staying with me temporarily until I can locate her mother, and Cap was a rescue dog. I've been busy with work, and haven't had the time to train either one of them."

"The girl's discipline is all on you." Twila's silver eyebrows shot upward. "But it just so happens I was once employed as a dog trainer. Would you like me to work with him?"

Bexley's shoulders rolled forward. "In addition to your going rate, I'll pay you in tears of gratitude."

"Neither will be necessary. I'll take payment in the form of you allowing me to fix up your landscaping. It's obvious you don't have a green thumb, and no one should be forced to eyeball that hot mess when they're out for a peaceful stroll on the beach. I figure a pop of color around that lovely shade of blue would be ideal."

Eying the sad little patch of bushes surrounding the cottage, Bexley knew there was no sense in arguing. Brewer had worked hard on restoring the cottage. It deserved greenery just as stunning.

"I'll stop by at first light to get Cap. We'll spend tomorrow getting to know each other until you return from work." Taking a swig of Bexley's Prosecco, Twila wiggled her eyebrows as she walked backwards. "I'll take this as payment for the flowers. Stop by if there's anything else I can do to help you spruce up the place before that handsome fella of yours returns home."

Bexley watched the woman waltz away, almost as if to a silent melody, and muttered, "What just happened?"

CHAPTER SIX

The following morning, Bexley ran by the office, then paid a visit to the Renners' remarkable mansion of concrete and glass overlooking Papaya Springs beach. It could've been more accurately described as an estate the way the monstrosity stretched out as far as the eye could see, forming a W-shape among well-groomed tennis courts and numerous pools. A dwelling that size seemed excessive for a family of four. Each of them could have their own wing and never run into each other.

"Miss Squires! Please come in." In a red silk robe, golden hair piled in a nest on her head, Sylvia ushered Bexley inside the double front doors to a grand foyer several stories high.

"Good morning, Mrs. Renner."

From the size of the bags under Sylvia's eyes, Bexley wondered if she'd slept at all since Teddy's accident. "You've found something to vindicate my son," she assumed.

"I'm sorry, but I don't have anything substantial to tell you at this point. I'm wondering if I could have a few minutes alone with your daughter. She might know something about Teddy's personal life that she wouldn't feel comfortable mentioning in front of her parents."

A young platinum blonde ambled into the room behind Sylvia, scrutinizing Bexley from head to toe with sharp blue eyes a shade lighter than the Pacific Ocean. With fierce cheekbones that could cut glass and a knockout figure in a cropped PSC t-shirt and micro shorts that made *Bexley* feel like the sixteen year old in the room, it seemed logical Mrs. Renner had mentioned her daughter expressed an interest in modeling.

The girl lifted her perfectly arched eyebrows. "Who're you?"

Sylvia attempted a polite smile. "This is Bexley Squires, the private investigator we hired to look into Teddy's…situation. Bexley, this is my daughter, Reese."

Reese lifted a single eyebrow a little higher and grinned. "A hot female PI? That's badass."

"I'm sorry about your brother," Bexley offered. "I'm doing my best to clear his name."

The teenager shrugged one shoulder. "It's whatever."

Sylvia's expression tightened with disapproval. "Reese, *sweetheart*, why don't you take Bexley out back to the main terrace while I have the staff whip you up some cinnamon apple Bostock and fresh lemon juice?"

Regarding her mother cautiously, as if being tested, Reese answered, "Okay?" and turned to Bexley, with a dramatic roll of her eyes. "This way."

Reese padded barefoot through the heart of their home to a concrete patio out back with elaborate cabanas, odd-shaped bushes, life-sized bronze statues emulating acting awards, and ample white sofas surrounding a massive pool. The space could've accommodated parties for several hundred guests.

Arms coiled around her tiny middle, Reese plopped down onto a couch and threw Bexley a curious look. "So what's this big secret you wanna ask without my mom around?"

Bexley sat across from her. "Do you know

anything about your brother possibly having a crush on a girl named Uma Trembly?"

"Nuh uh!" Giggling, Reese shook her head. "Where'd you hear that bogus rumor? There's no way he'd crush on her! He despises the space Uma occupies!"

Fred's story was becoming more transparent by the second. "Are you absolutely sure?"

"I'd bet my new Louis Vuittons on the fact that he would never give her, or anyone remotely *like* her, the time of day."

"Could they be casual friends?"

"I mean…I guess it's possible. Teddy sometimes brings home the weirdest people."

"Friends other than Dalton Hulbert and P.J. Howard?"

Reese shrugged. "Sometimes."

"Anyone new come around shortly before his accident? Anyone that maybe had a history of bullying, or known as a criminal?"

"You think he could've been holding onto the gun for someone else," Reese assumed. "Then what about the creepy notebook?"

Bexley tilted her head. "Your parents told you everything?"

"They told me there was a gun and a notebook

with a list of girls, and a map of the school with certain classrooms circled. They figured I should know all the details in case rumors started."

"What's your take on the situation?"

"I don't really know what to think." With a sniffle, Reese started picking at the peeling nail polish on her fingers. "Teddy's mental, but not that level of mental. He's smart. I can't see him planning… *you know*…and leaving evidence laying around. I don't think he hated anyone enough to do something that bad. Besides, he was really stoked about going off to college. He would've known something like that would've ended with him either in jail or dead."

Smart guy with a smart sister, Bexley thought. "Is Teddy well-liked at school?"

"For the most part. Some of the kids think he's a smart ass. I don't think he tries to be the way he is."

"Have you heard of any incidents of him being bullied by either classmates or teachers?"

"If anyone was bullying him, he'd just let it roll off his shoulders."

"Do you know anything about his history with Fred Finnegan?"

A nervous-sounding laugh burst from Reese's

generous lips. "Teddy and Mr. Fred *hate* each other. History lesson over."

"Are you sure there isn't anything more to it?"

"I don't know what else there could be. Mr. Fred's a super nice guy—everyone at the academy adores him." Reese's eyes skipped past Bexley to fix on the roaring ocean in the distance. "I don't understand why Teddy has a grudge against him."

"Can you tell me what kind of relationship Teddy has with Lexie Swenson?"

Reese's eyes darted back to Bexley. "I don't think they have any kind of *relationship*," Reese snapped. "She's besties with Uma." The girl stood. "Are we done now?"

Bexley slipped a business card from her handbag. "If you can think of anything else, please drop me a text or email. It's important that I know everything about your brother's relationships at school."

Nodding slightly, Reese turned the little card in her fingers. It seemed the questions about Teddy and Mr. Fred had made her sullen.

Bexley stood to leave. "One more thing. Do you know how I can get in touch with either Lexie or Uma?"

"What's your obsession with Uma?" Reese

demanded in a sour tone. "What does it matter whether or not she was friends with my brother?"

"Because that list your parents told you about? Uma was on it. Lexie too."

The girl suddenly turned as white as the couch behind her. "You think—"

"We can't assume anything until I have all the facts straight."

Reese's slender shoulders bowed inward. "No one knows what happened to Uma. She just…*disappeared* after the last day of school. There are rumors going around that she ran away."

Unease swept over Bexley. "I'd appreciate anything you can dig up for me. Her cell phone number, her parents' number or address— anything."

Bending the business card, Reese looked away. "I'll see what I can do."

By the time Bexley settled in behind her desk at Stronghold Investigations, she was oozing with frustration. Until she knew how to get in touch with Uma Trembly or the other girls on the list, she'd hit a dead end on Teddy's case. She decided if she didn't do something proactive, she'd lose her mind.

Twisting the *"be a quick wit"* pen from Cineste in her fingers, she made the decision to call her sister. "What are the chances I can get you to kid and dog sit for a few hours tonight?"

"Hot date?" Cineste teased.

"Yeah, with Brewer's GTO and the open road. I shouldn't be home too late."

"I'd pick them up at Temperance's place?"

"Yeah, but my weird neighbor lady took Cap for the day, so you'll just be picking up Olive. Think you could be there by six?"

"Are you kidding? I'm dying to see how that woman lives with my own eyes."

"Thanks, sis. I'll owe you one."

"Perfect, because I need your advice on something. I'll go into the details when you get back."

Bexley wasn't convinced she was in a position to give anyone advice on literally *anything*, but she'd deal with the issue later. After debriefing Red and letting Temperance know her sister would be by later, she slid into Brewer's sleek black classic 2-door, taking a minute to appreciate the dark rumble of the engine. Being surrounded by the rich scent of leather and knowing Brewer had spent precious time restoring the car to its original beauty was almost as good as having him along for the ride.

Long before the noon hour crowd clogged the interstate, she was headed east. With Hozier's newest album playing from the updated car stereo, it seemed as if she'd breached the Arizona border in no time. It was mid-afternoon when she parked outside of Linda Roberts's place in a park several dozen trailers deep.

The desert's dry heat sizzled against her skin the moment she stepped outside to assess her surroundings, handbag draped across her torso. Patches of dead grass surrounded the army green structure that couldn't have been more than 30 feet long. It was hard to determine where their yard ended and the surrounding neighbors' began as they were all piled with junk cars, ATVs, and mopeds.

From a faded set of lawn chairs arranged on a ratty old rug beneath the trailer's awning, a younger man and older woman watched Bexley closely. Though Sadie's mother appeared several years older than the mugshots Red had provided, there was no mistaking it was the same woman. Honey-blond curls had been replaced with a drab, washed-out gray mess, and the deep lines of crow's feet around her eyes were a stark white in comparison to her deeply tanned face. Her nut-brown eyes didn't stray from Bexley as she slurped from a can of beer, then rested the can on her generous chest barely contained in a see-through tank top over a bright pink bra. With a chill, Bexley noted numerous needle marks in the woman's arm.

"That's a mighty nice car ya got there," the younger man commented, his voice thick with a southern accent. He spewed a mouthful of tobacco off to the side before producing a can of chew from the pocket of his torn t-shirt. Based on his round cheeks and smooth lips, Bexley guessed him to be in his early to mid thirties. Pretty green eyes and a generous head of dark hair placed him somewhere in-between handsome and detrimental on the eyes. As he stuffed his bottom lip with more tobacco, his gaze lazily skimmed over Bexley's body. "She's a real beauty."

Swallowing the need to vomit, Bexley addressed the woman. "Linda Roberts?"

"We ain't got no money to buy whatever yer sellin'," Linda snarled, "so ya may as well turn yer pretty little self back around and leave."

Still hesitant, Bexley inched a bit closer. Neither Linda nor her boyfriend cast a welcoming look, and both sets of eyes appeared slightly dilated. "I'm here to ask you a few questions about your daughter."

Linda guffawed, revealing a mouth void of teeth. "What's that worthless girl done now?"

"She took off and left Olive behind."

"Don't surprise me any," Linda said, waving a hand through the air. "She ain't fit to be a momma."

The man scowled. "You with child services? Ya look more like a cop."

Bexley continued to ignore him. "I'm wondering if you have any idea where I could find Sadie."

"Ya might wanna start with the strip clubs." Taking another drink of her beer, Linda grunted. "If she's not there, ya can probably find her some-where behind bars. She's always pullin' a scam on someone, somewhere. Only a matter of time before she's locked up for good."

As sweat dribbled down Bexley's back, she refused to accept she'd made the four-plus hour trip for nothing. "Do you know of anyone specifically she may be running from...or maybe even *with*?"

"Could be anyone she's ever come in contact with," Linda told her. She crushed the empty can of beer in her fingers and tossed it into a pile of more cans beside her bare feet. "She's made herself a lotta enemies over the years."

"When did you speak with her last?"

"I don't know. Months? Years?" Linda pulled a pack of cigarettes out from her bra and began packing it against the palm of her hand. "Me and her ain't exactly friendly."

Sucking down a deep breath, Bexley asked, "Who's Sadie's father? Maybe he'd know how to get in touch with her."

"Bastard's no longer with us," Linda said, grunting. "Pro'ly a good thing, 'cause he was a bad man…that's for damn sure."

Panic slipped over Bexley's heart. Her father had made his share of mistakes, but were they enough to qualify him as a "bad" man? It certainly wasn't enough to confirm or deny the Captain had been Sadie's father. "She was receiving money from a man out in California," she prodded. "Someone named Dominic Ferguson. Was that him?"

Linda's eyes narrowed. "How'd you know about that?"

"I'm a private investigator."

"My Sadie…she's a sly one, but I guess not sly enough." Stopping to light her cigarette, Linda puffed on it, then grinned. "One night I told 'er I'd slept with a Navy man before she was born—back when I was a dancer—and I seen him in the news not too long ago for bein' some high flutin' officer. She tracked 'im down and made 'im believe he was her daddy. First I figured it was wishful thinkin' on her part, that she wanted a good man to be her daddy, then I realized she's just a professional con-artist, just like her *real* daddy who spent more than half his life in prison."

Air whooshed back into Bexley's lungs. *Sadie wasn't her sister*. Her instincts had been right all along. But where did that leave Olive? She felt an unexpected rush of sadness. "What about Olive's father? Do you know how I can get in touch with him?"

"Don't know who he is…neither does Sadie. Could be any one'a the johns she's slept with. Ya could try enterin' the kid's DNA into the system, see which felon comes up." Tipping her head back, Linda cackled.

Bexley dug her fingernails into the palms of her hands, cringing. She was beginning to get a clearer picture of Olive's life, and it wasn't pretty. "If Sadie doesn't come back soon, Olive could end up in the system."

Linda took a long drag of her cigarette. "What do ya care where she goes?" Smoke burst from her narrow nostrils. "Who're you?"

"And why you drivin' a car with California plates?" the boyfriend added.

Bexley decided it wasn't a good time to disclose her personal interest in the matter. She'd trust a crazed rapper as the next POTUS before she'd trust the boyfriend. "I was hired to track Sadie down."

The boyfriend grunted. "Hired by that uptight lady from Minnesota?"

Bexley finally turned to face him, wincing with the suggestive look he was throwing her. "What lady?"

"Some *friend*," he hooked quotations with his fingers, "of Sadie's. She came here a few days ago askin' questions, same as you. Doubt they were as close as she claimed—wore a fancy suit, drove a Mercedes. Not the type to be hangin' around Sadie. Not on purpose."

Hope sparked in Bexley. Maybe Sadie was hiding from someone important. "Did this woman give you a phone number, or some other way to get in touch with her?"

With a sickening grin, the boyfriend rose to his feet and staggered Bexley's way. He stopped uncomfortably close, lifting his chin, clouding her with the stench of body odor and tobacco. "How much is it worth to ya?"

CHAPTER SEVEN

By the time Bexley rolled into her driveway behind Cineste's Acura, the ocean was nothing more than a peaceful dark shadow off in the distance. With relief rolling off her shoulders, she killed the engine. After paying Linda's boyfriend the hundred and thirty dollars she had on her in cash, she peeled rubber out of there, grateful to leave them behind in the rearview mirror. Although she felt a lingering guilt for riding Brewer's GTO so hard, she'd rather deal with the consequences for any possible damage before she wanted to explain to him how she'd walked into yet another situation she shouldn't have faced alone. For a stuttered heartbeat, she feared Linda and her boyfriend would forcefully steal the car and do away with her.

She retrieved the business card they'd handed over. The only information printed on the plain white card was a name in black, bold print: SUMMER LANDRY. A phone number with a 612 area code was scrawled beneath it in blue pen with nearly perfect penmanship. Bexley had only called the number once since leaving Arizona as it was a Minnesota number, and she assumed no one would answer her call at the late hour. A quick internet search of Summer's name hadn't provided anything tangible aside from a few business profiles that may or may not have been the woman in question.

With the sudden sound of knuckles tapping on her window, she shrieked. Cineste bent down to her eye level, bottle of Bexley's favorite Prosecco in hand.

"YOU'RE ABSOLUTELY POSITIVE SADIE'S NOT OUR sister?" Cineste repeated. With one arm wrapped around her knees, blanket pulled up to her neck, her eyes fixed on the dark ocean beneath the star-filled sky. She had patiently listened as Bexley recapped her impromptu trip to Arizona, but she'd squirmed the entire time. "I can't say I'm sad about it, but I am ticked that she took advantage of Dad like that. Are you sure her mom wasn't too drunk to know what she was talking about?"

"At this point? There's only one way to be absolutely certain of the truth." Bexley took a sip of Prosecco before leaning back to enjoy the slight burn of alcohol sliding down into her stomach. Part of her felt a tinge of guilt for drinking alone, but she deserved it after the harrowing road trip. It wasn't her fault that her sister didn't appreciate a good glass of sparkling wine. "We could send in a sample of Olive's DNA to get tested."

Cineste stroked the sleeping dog snuggled between the sisters on the outdoor sofa, and let out a long breath. "That little girl is so sweet...and funny...and *brave*. What if she's not really our niece? We can't just send her back to Minnesota. They'll either throw her in the system, or she'll go back to sleeping on pool toys in random men's houses with her mom." She glanced back at the dark cottage, wiggling her toes out from beneath the blanket before lowering her voice. "I worry it'll crush her if she discovers she isn't really a part of our family."

"She wouldn't have to know. We can take a sample of her hair while she's asleep. Even if she's not blood related, no one says we have to send her away." When the dog stretched a little, nudging Bexley's thigh, she scratched behind his ear. "I spoke with Luke on the drive back. Family law isn't his specialty, but he thinks we'll have several options that will depend on whether or not we can find Sadie. We can hire an attorney who's experienced in this kind of thing to advocate for Olive's well-being, and ensure she's placed in a good home. We just won't have much of a say as to where she'll end up unless we give the court viable options for placement."

"I can't foster her," Cineste blurted. "I mean, I'd love to and I wish I could, but…" She sat tall, letting the blanket slide down her shoulders. The fluttery pink tank top she wore with a pattern of tiny little hearts was fun and flirty—a perfect match to Cineste's personality. Her eyes watered as she attempted a shaky smile. "I'm pregnant, Bex."

Bexley's mouth dropped open. Her baby sister was going to be a mom? It would've surprised her far less if Ashton Kutcher had emerged from the ocean and announced she was being punked.

Before Alex, Bexley wouldn't have trusted her moderately spoiled sister to keep a plant alive. But after being forced into sex trafficking and the drug rehab that followed, she had matured considerably.

Bexley snapped her jaw shut before her lips parted a second time. "Wha—how? How did that happen?"

"Well, Bex, when two people love each other—"

"Now who's the quick wit?" Bexley grumbled. "I *meant* how could you have been so careless?"

"Careless?" Cineste shot to her feet, scowling. "You say that like being pregnant with Alex's baby is a bad thing."

"That's not what I meant, Cin. It's just…you're both still in school, working part time, and barely making enough to keep your heads above water. We both know it's not cheap living in Papaya Springs. Brewer and I never would've been able to afford a place like this without the success of our two businesses. How are you and Alex going to provide for a baby?"

"We'll figure it out. Alex has been talking about starting a family for months now. It's just…I'm sure he'll be surprised it happened so soon. He'll come up with a plan so we can get by."

It was Bexley's turn to scowl. "You haven't told him?"

"That's actually the piece of advice I was fishing

for." Cineste lowered back down to the sofa and flicked her bottom lip through her teeth. The light went out of her eyes. "Do you think I should wait a little while before giving him the news? With Mom's history of miscarriages, I hate to get him all excited for nothing."

Bexley pressed her fingertips against her eyelids. She remembered all too well how their mother had been over-the-moon excited the two times she'd discovered she was pregnant with boys, and the grief that came later with losing them. It was one of many reasons why Bexley had never been excited by the idea of motherhood.

She glanced back at Cineste. "What does your doctor say?"

"I haven't seen one yet. I just took a drug store test a few days ago."

With an internal sigh, Bexley gave her sister a reassuring smile. If she ever had that kind of scare, she didn't know what she'd do. Having Olive around had only proved the life of a private investigator didn't leave much room for quality family time. "I'd start with a trip to an OBGYN and go from there. Maybe it's too soon to start worrying. I mean there is such a thing as a false positive."

"Maybe you're right," Cineste agreed in a quiet voice.

As Bexley watched her sister, her heart twisted. Although she knew Cineste would be okay no matter the outcome, she still worried. Cap groaned and stretched his legs, letting them dangle over the sofa. "What did Twila do to him?" she asked, stroking the dog's head.

Cineste giggled. "I don't know, but he's been like that ever since she brought him back. Maybe she let him run until he was too exhausted to move."

Bexley reached out to squeeze her sister's shoulder. "Everything will work out, Cin."

THE OCEAN WAS JUST AS DARK THE FOLLOWING morning when Bexley slipped out the backdoor of the cottage with her phone and a stainless steel bottle of water, dressed for her morning jog. She had altered her routine, practically running the beach in circles so she wouldn't be far from where Olive slept. For the first time since Cap had come to live with them, *she* had to wake *him*. It was downright comical how much Twila had worn him down.

After she stretched her limbs and let the dog do his business on the designated patch of grass in their backyard, she redialed the number on Summer Landry's business card. A crisp chill rolled off the calm body of water in front of her as sea gulls soared in dizzying patterns overhead. The best part about living beside a cliff was the fact that joggers rarely ventured that far down the beach. It was calm and peaceful, the way Bexley preferred.

"Summer Landry," a smooth female voice lulled with an air of boredom.

Bexley stood tall. "Hi, Ms. Landry. My name is Bexley Squires. I'm a private investigator from Papaya Springs, California, hired to locate Sadie Roberts. After a conversation with her mother, I understand you may have a shared interest in her whereabouts."

The tone in the woman's voice brightened. "Why on earth would someone in California be looking for Sadie?"

"The estate of a man she once conned is considering pressing charges, and possibly seeking restitution." It was a struggle to keep the bitterness out of her voice. She truly wished she could recover the money Sadie had swindled from their father when he'd been alive. It was too late to make things right with the Captain, but she wouldn't be opposed to creating a trust fund for Olive.

"Oh goodness," Summer said. "She *conned* someone?"

"How do you know Ms. Roberts?"

"Sadie was my office administrator before she vanished."

Bexley nearly choked as she took a swig of her water. Were they talking about the same Sadie Roberts? Based on the false IDs Bexley had found in her home, Sadie didn't seem capable of maintaining an honest office job. Bexley coughed a little before asking, "How long has she worked for you?"

"She was coming up on her one-year anniversary."

Interesting, Bexley thought. "What type of business do you run, Ms. Landry?"

"A professional matchmaking service. Aphrodite's Select is number one in Minnesota."

After the comment Linda had made about her daughter having "johns," Bexley sensed "matchmaking" was code for "escort," and Sadie was more than an administrator. It was more believable that Summer was a pimp who had lost control rather than a concerned employer. "When did you last speak with her?"

Summer forced a sigh. "I believe it was a week ago last Monday. I remember because she skipped out before dealing with payroll."

"Did she seem out of character that day?"

"Not that I noticed. She's quiet for the most part…keeps to herself."

"Do you or any of her coworkers have an inkling as to where she may have gone?"

"Like I said, she's quiet. She's never been close with the rest of my staff. As for myself, I don't know a single thing about her personal life. I wasn't even aware she had a child until I paid a visit to her mother."

"How did you find Linda Roberts?"

"Sadie listed her as an emergency contact."

"You must be incredibly worried about Sadie to have made the trip all the way down to Arizona."

"She's a valued employee."

Bexley could almost *smell* the woman's lies. "If you're not close with Sadie, why did you tell her mother that you're a friend rather than her employer?"

"I don't remember saying such a thing. I tried getting in touch with Linda Roberts several times via the number Sadie provided, but no one would return my call. Since the police seemed uninterested in treating it as a missing persons case, I decided it was necessary to take the matter into my own hands. No one else seemed to care that she'd gone missing."

"Sounds like something a friend would do," Bexley commented. Cap trotted over to her, nuzzling the back of her knee. "Ms. Landry, if you can think of anything that might be helpful in locating Sadie—"

"I'd like to contribute to your fees in tracking her down. Would ten thousand dollars be enough?"

Bexley flinched as she petted the dog's head. It was an extremely generous offer from a complete stranger. "You don't know anything about me. Maybe I'm simply pretending to be a private investigator."

"I'm looking at your firm's website as we speak. It appears you have strong, viable credentials. I remember hearing something about a female P.I. when Dean Halliwell was arrested for murder. You seem attentive to detail, and ask the right questions. I'll send you my email address, and you can forward a contract with the terms and conditions of your services."

While the offer was tempting, Bexley worried it was skirting on the edge of unethical. She had begun the search because she had a personal interest in finding Sadie. Then again, she had taken Olive in because of some misplaced loyalty to her father, thinking Sadie had been his kin, but that no longer applied. Bexley's own self-interest wouldn't conflict with Ms. Landry's if she took her on as a client. She wanted Sadie found so she could be made accountable and pay for her crimes.

The retainer could be applied toward any expenses incurred in Bexley's search, and her hourly rate could be set aside for Olive. The poor kid was going to need some kind of financial support if her mom had truly abandoned her.

"Ms. Landry, I'm not completely sure—"

"I'll look forward to hearing back from you, Miss Squires."

The call ended.

CHAPTER EIGHT

Something was notably different about Brewer when he came into view on the jailhouse monitor. "Good morning, gorgeous." There was an added brightness to his smile and boundless energy behind his greeting. He possessed the kind of playful air that reminded Bexley of the time he first let her know he was interested in more than her friendship. "I really dig that color on you. But you could wear a white pillow case and it'd look good."

"Mornin', big guy." Bexley's heart fluttered as she tugged on the lapel of the mustard blazer worn over a black button-down. The outfit, paired with black jeans and pointed flats, had magically appeared in her closet one recent morning. Not surprisingly, the attached tags were from Kiersten's favorite boutique. "Was there any coffee in your sugar this morning?"

The rich sound of his laughter made her grin from ear to ear. "Maybe I'm just having a good morning."

"Because they promised an extra minute of time in the yard? Something big put an extra slide in your jailhouse shuffle. Spill it, mister."

"Can't get anything past my girl." His eyes briefly skipped over the guard behind her. "Everything's good, babe. *Real* good." Suddenly somber, he scratched the scruff on his thick jaw. "When's the last time you talked to Luke?"

Her curiosity was officially triggered. The switch in conversation was intentional, and she couldn't recall him ever calling her *babe*. He was being cheeky for a reason. What did he know that he didn't want to discuss in front of the jailer? She couldn't wait to give Luke a call.

"As a matter of fact, I spoke with him last night," she answered. "I called to get his lawyerly advice on what our options are with Olive." She wished she could reach through the monitor to feel the comfort of his hand wrapped around hers. "The Captain wasn't Sadie's father, Hawk. I went to visit her mom in Arizona. She told me Sadie sought him out after her mom saw him in the news, and mentioned she'd once slept with him during her days as a stripper. Sadie's real father was a con artist, just like her."

"I'm sorry, B. I figured you were right about her, but I didn't want to accept that someone was taking advantage of you and your family." His eyebrows lifted. "Have you told Olive?"

"No, and I don't plan to until we have a solid plan in place. Cin and I decided to run a DNA test on her since Sadie's mom was drunk and possibly high on something when we spoke. No way I'm making any decisions based on that woman's word. I ran a sample of Olive's hair up to the diagnostic center on my way here. However this ends, I'm going to make damn sure she's in a good place. And I can promise you it won't be with her flake of a mother or her grandmother."

Holding his hand over his heart, Brewer winked several times. Yearning to feel his arms around her, she winked back.

LEXIE SWENSON, THE SECOND PERSON ON TEDDY Renner's list, was a stunning young woman. She sat on a bench overlooking the beach, golden brown hair spilling over her freckled shoulders in springy curls, held back by a pair of dark sunglasses perched on top of her head. The sharp slope of her button nose and narrowness of her cheeks gave her a fairy-like appearance. Dark blue eyes dominating a petite face watched Bexley carefully behind a veil of long, thick lashes that brushed over the apples of her cheeks with every blink. The sun's rays were already potent, making the girl look out of place in an oversized camo t-shirt that stopped several inches above her deeply tanned knees. Everyone else within eyesight wore swim wear, or at the most, bright coverups. The only bright thing on Lexie were her several carat diamond earrings and the red designer purse hooked over one shoulder.

"Lexie?"

The girl nodded. As Bexley took a seat on the bench beside her, Lexie watched as her fingers toyed with the hem of the oversized shirt. "I only agreed to this because Reese said you're cool, and I feel bad about her brother." Her voice sounded weak to Bexley's ears—almost like someone in mourning. "I don't know why you wanted to talk to me though."

Based on the list of grievances Teddy had listed

on her in the notebook, Bexley had been expecting a girl with a sharp tongue and a flippant attitude. She was slightly thrown off guard by her quiet innocence.

"I'm meeting with a handful of Teddy's peers and teachers to see if they can shed any light on his situation before the accident."

Lexie's eyes grew wide. "You mean, like, someone hit him on purpose, or he tried to commit suicide?"

"No, nothing like that." Though she wasn't willing to divulge anything more, Bexley was relieved to hear Reese must not've shared any information about the notebook or gun with Lexie. "Is he a friend of yours?"

"Hardly," Lexie answered with a snigger. Her eyes returned to her shirt. "I know I shouldn't say this about someone in his condition, but he could be a real jerk."

"Did you have any classes together?"

"Just, like, a couple last year, and one this year."

"Did you talk to him much?"

"Not really. Last semester in AP English, Mr. Fred assigned us and Uma to the same group. We talked about our project, but that was it."

"Reese said you and Uma are close. Do you know how I can get in touch with her?"

Lexie squirmed against the bench, adjusting her legs. "She's…um…spending some time at her grandparents' place in Anaheim. She went through some stuff this year."

"Anything involving Teddy?"

"What?" Lexie's large eyes met Bexley's gaze, and she sneered. "No! Ew! Why would you think that?"

"Because Teddy's parents have reason to believe there was something serious going on with him, and the only helpful information I've been able to gather so far involves him arguing with Uma in AP English. Is there anything useful you can tell me?"

"Teddy's…Teddy. He thinks he's better than everyone else because he's so stinking smart. I wouldn't doubt it if someone was giving him a hard time for being so cocky."

"Anyone in particular?"

"Not really, but the guys into sports have always despised him."

"Did you ever see Teddy and Uma arguing in AP English, or would you have any idea why they weren't getting along?"

"I didn't see it, but it doesn't surprise me. Like everyone else, she thinks he's super annoying."

"They're not friends either?"

"No way."

"What about the teachers? From what you'd seen, did they treat him differently?"

"I don't know…I guess…maybe."

"Had you ever noticed whether or not he got along with Mr. Fred?"

"Not really." Lexie's eyes returned to her fingers on her shirt. "Have you talked to P.J. and Dalton? They'd know more about Teddy than anyone."

"I haven't been able to get in touch with them either. They won't return my calls, and no one answered the door when I stopped by their houses."

"That's because their parents are in Greece for the summer."

"Their families are close?"

Lexie lifted one shoulder. "I guess. I've heard they always go on trips together."

"Where do P.J. and Dalton stay while their parents are gone?"

"Dalton's parents have a second place on the beach. They've been throwing big parties every night since graduation."

"No one likes Teddy, but they like his friends?"

"The kids from our school pretend to like anyone with a sick pad, offering free booze. Doesn't mean P.J. and Dalton are popular."

"Any chance you can give me the address to that place on the beach?"

Wrapping her arms around her waist, Lexie frowned. "Are you going to, like, bust them for drinking?"

"I'm not a cop, Lexie. I simply need to speak with them."

"I don't know the exact address, but I guess I could give you directions. I've heard they're throwing a party tomorrow night…with a deejay." She gave Bexley a sharp look. "But I'll only tell you where it is if you promise you won't tell anyone I'm the one who ratted them out."

"I won't say a word," Bexley vowed. "What about Uma? Do you suppose you could convince her to return my calls?"

"I can try, but no promises there. She hasn't exactly been herself lately."

"Lexie, what kind of stuff did she go through?"

The girl's gaze shifted to several kids building a sandcastle nearby. "It's not my business to say. You'll have to ask her yourself."

L UKE AND K IERSTEN PULLED INTO THE DRIVEWAY seconds behind Bexley and Olive. Olive climbed out of the SUV and stood watching their guests with one hand on her hip. "Is this *another* aunt of mine, or another one of your movie star friends?"

As Kiersten and Luke moved toward them with takeout bags from Pollo's in hand, still dressed to the nines in work attire, Bexley laughed. "You can call her Auntie if you'd like—she's basically family. This is my friend Kiersten, and her fiancé Luke. Guys, this little ball of fire is Olive."

"It's so nice to meet you, Olive!" Kiersten gushed, bending to give her a formal handshake. "Welcome to California!"

Olive titled her head. "Are you an actress?"

"She'd put everyone in Hollywood to shame," Luke interjected with a laugh. He gathered the bags in one hand and slid his other arm around Kiersten's shoulders. "Nice to meet you, little lady."

Bexley spun toward the cottage, motioning for everyone to follow. "Come—whoa!" The new sweep of color and different textures surrounding the little cottage in various plants and flowers took her breath away. Their vibrance was enough to give the building a freshly painted look, yet it somehow flowed perfectly with the relaxed vibe of the ocean beyond. "Either my neighbor was here today, or I've been visited by landscaping fairies."

"Wow," Kiersten gasped beside her. "Who's this neighbor? Joanna Gaines?"

"No, but I'm starting to think this woman could be her mother. Lets go check it out."

Handing her share of the takeout bags over to Luke, Kiersten stood on the balls of her designer stilettos to kiss his cheek. "Would you be so kind as to get the plates and silverware ready for us, sweet future husband of mine?"

Rolling her eyes, Olive waved him toward the front door. "Come on, Luke. I'll show you where everything is."

Kiersten watched him hustle to keep up with Olive before they disappeared inside the house. "She really is a spit fire, Bex." Lowering her voice, she giggled. "Are you sure she's not a blood relative?"

"I honestly wish she was."

Kiersten hooked her arm through Bexley's as they rounded the side of the cottage to investigate the landscaping. Twila kneeled over a bag of soil in a floral kimono and costume jewelry as vivid as the flowers she'd planted. Once again, her hair was styled in a single braid that flowed down her slender back. Cap sat calmly at her side, watching with rapt attention.

Kiersten nudged Bexley. "Who is this magical creature, and how much will she charge to be the florist for my wedding?"

With a tinkling laugh, Twila slowly rose to her feet. "That would be too big of a job for an old crow like me." She spun around to face them with a sweet smile. "Good evening, Bexley and—"

"Kiersten Douglas," Bexley answered. "Kiersten, this is my neighbor, Twila Finn. After Olive and Cap destroyed her prized roses, Twila decided the best course of action would be to transform my cottage into less of an eye-sore."

Kiersten rushed forward to shake Twila's hand. "It's a pleasure to meet you, Miss Finn! You've done a *spectacular* job! And to think you did this out of the kindness of your heart—"

"Not at all," Twila replied, smiling. "I'll be billing Miss Squires for the cost of the flowers *and* my time." She retrieved a small object from the pocket on her white jeans and threw it for Cap to catch in his mouth. "Good boy, Cap. Okay!"

As if Cap had been released from a chain, he

left the woman's side and trotted over to greet Bexley. Laughing, she squatted down to let him lick her face as she eyed Twila. "Are you going to clue me in on what I bought?"

Twila gestured toward a bush of stunning red flowers. "The Midnight Marvel hibiscus will come back every year along with the blue and white Hardy Everblooming Geranium mix. The lavender will provide a lovely fragrance, and the Sweet Williams are a delight to behold once they're in full bloom. I planted a few annuals on the street side that you'll have to replace next spring."

Bexley nodded along, dumfounded. She'd never remember the names of the flowers, and she didn't have any idea what an "annual" looked like.

Twila gestured to the front of the cottage. "Since your man is a veteran, I added some dusty miller for a subtle patriotic color scheme without making it too gaudy."

"Hold on." Standing upright, Bexley shook her head and frowned. "I never told you Brewer was a veteran."

"You didn't?" Twila's thin shoulders lifted. "Well, I have been told I possess a touch of psychic abilities."

Kiersten held the back of her hand up to her

mouth. "Maybe you should add those services to the bill."

"Don't encourage her," Bexley grumbled, elbowing Kiersten. She was beginning to suspect Twila hadn't wandered into her life by accident. Would Brewer have been sneaky enough to hire the woman to keep an eye on her? "You did all of this just today *and* trained my dog to behave?"

"So far I've only trained Cap how to sit, stay, and come when called. Tomorrow we'll work on heeling so he isn't all over the place when you go for your morning jog. He has a long way to go yet, but he's a good dog. He's eager to please, so long as you have a pocket full of treats. He prefers organic."

Bexley felt a sudden urge to hug the woman, but resisted. "Thank you, Twila. Really. The house looks amazing." She felt a rush of warmth when picturing Brewer first laying eyes on the much needed update. "Brewer is going to love what you've done."

"Of course he will," Twila answered smartly. She wiped her forearm over her forehead and grinned. "Ladies, I believe I hear a long, hot shower calling my name." Tucking what was left of the soil under her arm, she held Bexley's gaze. "I'll be back same time tomorrow to get Cap. I'll show you how to care for everything some other time when you don't have company."

"Thank you!" Bexley repeated as the woman waltzed away.

"So nice to meet you!" Kiersten called out before turning to Bexley. "What a gem she is!" Grinning, she squeezed Bexley's biceps. "We better hurry and eat before our dinner gets cold. Then Luke can fill you in on Brewer."

CHAPTER NINE

While Bexley and her friends settled on the furniture in her backyard, Cap barked behind Olive, chasing the droplets of water that flicked off her bare feet.

Luke sat with one arm slung around Kiersten as they both sipped on glasses of Lambrusco. "They certainly get along well," he commented, gesturing to the dog and girl.

"*Luke!*" Bexley scolded, setting her glass on the end table. "I'm *literally* going to implode if you don't tell me—"

"Brewer has a good shot at being released early," he blurted. "I'll be able to tell you with absolute certainty after I meet with the county prosecutor next week."

Tears sprung to Bexley's eyes as she absorbed what he was saying. *Brewer was getting out early.*

A sly grin slipped over Kiersten's lips. "Told you it was good."

"W-what happened?" Bexley stammered. "How early?"

Luke's grin grew wider than Kiersten's. "Do you remember when you were trying to convince Vinnie Romano not to shoot Mattia Ricci, and Vinnie mentioned that Mattia had been running a scheme for Mayor Hoffman?"

"I couldn't forget that showdown even if I tried." Mayor Hoffman and famed mobster Mattia Ricci were both rotting in their respective cells because of Bexley's best efforts. "What does that have to do with shortening Brewer's sentence?"

"He's been keeping a close ear on things since he went in. He overheard some inmates talking about details Mattia had shared when they were bunkmates, and Mattia was awaiting his trial. He was funneling drug money for the mayor under the guise of a dry cleaning business in exchange for a thirty percent cut."

"Of course he was," Bexley grumbled.

"I let the prosecutor know Brewer had valuable information on the mayor's operation, and asked for a deal in exchange for the details. She was quite interested—said we could work something out."

Swallowing the lump in her throat, Bexley stood and launched herself at Luke, kissing him squarely on the lips. "You're the best, Luke Jacobs! If you weren't marrying my best friend, I'd get down on one knee right this second and beg you to be mine."

Luke wiggled his eyebrows teasingly. "I could always make you two sister wives."

"I'd like to see you run that idea by Brewer," Kiersten said with a snorting giggle.

Bexley tried to calm her thudding heart. It was best not to get too excited in case the deal fell through. But still…she couldn't stop herself from grinning at her friends like a lovesick fool.

<hr>

THE NEXT EVENING AFTER AN UNEVENTFUL DAY OF searching for leads on Sadie—mostly because Bexley was too caught up in daydreams involving Brewer's return home—she arranged for Cineste to watch Olive so she could follow Lexie's directions to Dalton and P.J.'s party. After slipping $40 to the underage "bouncer" guarding the set of double doors leading into the extravagant beach house, she mingled among scores of inebriated juveniles in various stages of undress. Based on a quick search she'd made on the academy's website, she was able to locate the hosts at the far edge of the pool within seconds.

The two friends stood like a couple of peacocks, watching on with animated laughter and wide smiles. They each wore obnoxiously printed Hawaiian shirts and dark swim trunks.

Dalton, the taller of the two boys, left his shirt unbuttoned to showcase a scrawny torso covered in bright red lipstick kisses. He drank straight from a liter-sized bottle filled with amber liquid. His broad face was ruddy and he swayed on his feet. Eyes the same shade as his generous copper hair glistened beneath the string of lights crisscrossing all over the backyard.

P.J., a strawberry blond with wavy locks down past his ears, was nearly as wide as he was tall. With a Solo cup clenched in one hand and a lit cigar in the other, he watched the hundreds of partygoers dancing to the techno tune with a proud, yet sober expression. A stain of red liquid covered his stout belly, and his complexion gave off a waxy sheen.

As Bexley assessed the scantily dressed girls around her, she decided her sister's advice on what to wear in order to blend in with a high school crowd had been spot-on. She crossed her arms over the low-cut crop-top when Dalton sized her up with a mischievous grin.

"Good thing you're not dancing on a stage right now, sweetheart," he told her. "I'd go broke—without question."

Casting him a pitiful glare, Bexley shook her head. "Better work on your pick-up lines before you leave for college in the fall, or you'll be starting classes with a nasty shiner." She stepped in between them, draping her arms around their shoulders. "This is quite the rager, boys. Did you blow your entire trust funds when bribing the neighbors into staying quiet, or did you save money for a few more keggers before your parents return from Greece?"

"Who are you?" P.J. demanded in a deep, rumbling voice. "Aren't you a little *old* to be crashing graduation parties?"

"Says one of two eighteen-year-olds throwing an alcohol-infused gathering," she quipped, letting her arms drop at her sides. "I'm willing to bet booze isn't the worst thing being indulged here tonight, either." When both boys blanched, she held up one hand. "Relax, boys. I'm only here because I'm hoping you can shed some light on Teddy's situation before the accident."

Dalton threw her a dark look. "You're that P.I. that keeps calling."

"Bingo. I wouldn't be here if you had bothered to return one of those calls." She forced out a breath. "Look…I won't bust your balls and report this little jamboree as long as you cooperate by answering my questions."

P.J. took a step forward, scowling. "That's bull—"

Dalton shoved him back and eyed Bexley. "What do you wanna know?"

"What's the connection between Teddy and Uma Trembly?" she asked. "Did he ever talk about her to either of you?"

The two boys fell silent as they exchanged a weary look.

"Do you have any idea how irate your parents would be if they had to fly *fifteen hours* just to bail you out of this mess?" Bexley asked, tapping Cineste's strappy stilettos against the concrete. "Come on, boys. Tell me what you know. Were Teddy and Uma enemies? Friends? *Lovers*?"

"He definitely didn't have a crush on her like

Mr. Fred made everyone believe," Dalton blurted. "Teddy was trying to…*help* her."

Bexley lifted her eyebrows. "Help her do what, exactly?"

"He wouldn't tell us—no matter how much shit we gave him." Dalton thrust a hand through his wild dark hair. "Whatever it was, it must've been a big deal. He's not one to keep secrets from us."

Still skeptical, Bexley studied the boy. "If Teddy was trying to help her, then why were they fighting in Mr. Fred's class?"

"No idea, but Teddy told me she changed her mind about wanting his help," P.J. answered, eyes cast downward. "He said he was going to do it anyway."

"Then he went off on how the less fortunate kids at the academy weren't treated the same as the rest of us," Dalton added.

"And Uma is one of them," Bexley concluded.

Dalton gave a reluctant nod. "Her parents aren't exactly poor, they just don't have a multi-million dollar mansion in Papaya Springs like everyone else. They live in a decent high-rise just outside of L.A. She went to the academy on a partial scholarship. Not a lot of people knew it until recently because she always pretended to be one of the rich ones."

Heart racing, Bexley sensed the truth was finally bubbling to the surface. "What happened recently?"

"She was basically ousted by her best friends for being…" he glanced over at P.J.

"A hoe," his friend finished.

Heat spread through Bexley's face. "That's not a nice word for a high school *girl*, boys." She clenched her jaw until the urge to zap them both with her stun gun passed. "I suspect your mothers taught you better."

"You asked!" P.J. snapped. "I'm just repeating the exact word her friends used!"

"He's not lying," Dalton said. "They were pretty ruthless."

Real life mean girls, Bexley thought bitterly. "Who are these 'friends'?"

P.J. shrugged. "Basically all the really popular girls at the academy. Maddi, Betsy, Kendall, Sarah, Addie, Lily, Ava, Lexie—"

"Lexie *Swenson*?" Bexley interrupted with a shiver. Every girl he'd named was listed in Teddy's notebook, and Lexie was allegedly Uma's best friend.

"Yeah." P.J. lifted the palms of his hands at his

sides. "Why does it matter? They were *all* total bitches to Uma. I don't know if she slept with one of their boyfriends or what, but they turned on her out of the blue."

"Don't forget Teddy's sister," Dalton said to him.

"You're saying *Reese* was one of them?" Bexley asked, thoroughly confused.

"She was probably the most ruthless one of all," Dalton confirmed, shrugging. "Rumor has it she's the one who spray painted nasty stuff on Uma's car and locker."

Reese had claimed she didn't know the reason why Uma had run off. Had she told Bexley *anything* truthful?

Bexley's eyes flickered between the two boys. "Do either of you know where I can find Uma? It's urgent that I have a chance to talk with her."

"Why?" P.J. challenged.

"Just trust me, P.J. Teddy's future may depend on it."

"Let me find my girlfriend," Dalton offered. "She'll know—she's one of the rare nice ones we graduated with. Brooke actually reached out to Uma to make sure she was okay after she took off. I think she was worried Uma would do something, you know, *bad*." He paused, his gaze sweeping over the rowdy crowd. "Hold on…I'll be right back."

As Dalton left in search of his girlfriend, Bexley pondered what way Teddy could've possibly helped Uma in her unfortunate situation. Had he planned to avenge her humiliation by punishing her friends—his own sister included?

As soon as Bexley arrived at Temperance's estate, she pulled her friend aside while Olive continued to chase Cinderella around the yard. Red had called on the way over to let her know she'd convinced the lab to push Olive's test through, and the results were ready to be picked up. Bexley had a sinking feeling things were about to propel into motion at a much faster rate once they knew the truth. "Thanks for letting her stay so late this time," she told Temperance.

Always the gracious host, Temperance made a shushing noise. "It's my pleasure to have her company."

Bexley's quit-witted way of thinking kicked in. "How would you feel about heading down to Anaheim with me and Olive tomorrow after I visit

Brewer? We could take her to the parks on Saturday—"

"Say no more," Temperance said right before a bright smile spread across her face. "The poor *niña* has been through too much for someone her age. I can only imagine her delight when we tell her where we're going. Leave the arrangements to me, *mi amiga*. I promise to make this weekend an experience neither of you will ever forget."

"Full disclosure," Bexley warned, "I'm going there with the hopes of interviewing someone on a case. Depending on what I discover, I can't promise I'll be able to stick around." She'd decided Uma might not be open to talking with her, and decided a surprise visit would be best. According to Dalton's girlfriend, Uma no longer kept any kind of social life and would likely be at her grandparents' on a Friday afternoon. "I sense I'm on the verge of uncovering some answers for the Renners."

"Always working," Temperance mused with a tick of her tongue. "And I promised your *novio* I'd take good care of you while he's away."

Warmth spread through Bexley's insides. Who *hadn't* Brewer requested to keep an eye on her before he'd left? While she didn't appreciate anyone doubting her capabilities to protect herself, somehow the gesture wasn't as threatening when coming from him.

She wrapped her fingers around Temperance's lean bicep. "And you haven't let him down, my friend. Just the opposite. Without knowing I can count on you to take good care of Olive, I wouldn't be able to do my job."

"Consider us even," Temperance said, patting Bexley's arm. "Without Ms. Olive in my life, I wouldn't wake every morning with a smile on my face."

Holding back a wince, Bexley dipped her chin with understanding. She had yet to tell Temperance that Olive was likely not her niece, and possibly wouldn't be sticking around for much longer. She sensed the sweet reality star would be devastated once Olive was sent away. But that was just another chore she'd have to put off until after she had found Sadie, and uncovered the truth from Uma Trembly.

CHAPTER TEN

"Luke and Kiersten came over for dinner the other night," Bexley announced the moment Brewer appeared on the monitor. "Even though they brought Pollo's, the conversation we had afterwards was far better."

A light filled his eyes as he settled into the chair, thick elbows on his knees. "God knows how much you love tacos from Pollo's."

Grinning, she shrugged. "Turns out there are actually some things I love even more."

With a giant smile, he held her stare for a gloriously long moment. While she feared she was letting herself get too excited when Luke had yet to seal the deal, she felt Brewer's love for her as much as she was projecting it back at him. Regardless of how much longer they'd be apart, she knew they'd survive and come out even stronger as a couple.

Wetting his lips with his tongue, he glanced at the skinny jeans and striped shirt she'd changed into. "You're looking rather casual today, B. You can't expect me to believe you actually took the day off."

"I'm headed to Anaheim with Temperance and Olive. Hopefully I'll meet with a key witness on a case tonight, and we'll hit the parks in the morning. Kiersten and Cineste are considering coming down with Luke and Alex to meet us."

He rubbed his chin and chuckled like he couldn't quite picture it. "Have to say I'm a little jealous. Bexley Squires in an amusement park? *Please* tell me you're buying a set of those cute little ears."

"*Maybe.*" She felt a tug of guilt for mentioning the whole crew was coming. But after she'd called both Kiersten and Cineste to fill them in on Olive's test results as well as their plans for the weekend, they had each invited themselves to come along. Besides, with any luck he'd be released soon. They could all return another time before Olive moved on to the next phase of her life. Feeling the burn of tears behind her eyelids, she blurted, "I got the results back on Olive's hair sample. She's not my niece, Hawk."

"You knew that was coming," he reminded her in a gentle voice.

"I know, but…it still sucks. I don't know how I'm going to tell Olive."

"Do I have to remind you yet again the kind of things you can accomplish?"

"No. And it was also unnecessary to recruit all of Papaya Springs to keep an eye on me."

"What do you mean?"

She rolled her eyes. "Temperance, Colt, the new neighbor lady…you probably brainwashed my sister and Kiersten too. I swear even the mailman looks at me with empathy, like my dog died or something."

His shoulders jiggled with a silent chuckle. "Can't say I know anything about a neighbor lady or the mailman, but I'm glad to hear they're all looking out for you. Have you stopped to consider they may be doing it on their own free will? You're a good person, B. You probably think I'm just biased, but I knew it was true long before I fell for you."

She blinked through a sudden onset of tears. "I miss you, Hawk. Not just for the reasons one would think. I miss the way you're always making jokes to keep me on my toes. I miss our meaningful talks. I miss your advice." She swiped at a tear right as it escaped her left eye. "Something about a case I'm working on has made me more uneasy than usual, and I hate that we don't know what's going to happen to Olive. Sometimes I can't deal with the ugly things I witness in this line of work. I need your wisdom more than ever."

"It kills me to hear you say that." He leaned in a little closer to the camera. "Just hang in there a little longer, B. Soon I'll be there for you just like before. There's only one thing I care about above everything else, and I'm not losing site of that ever again. Once I'm back, I'm not going anywhere."

Nodding through her tears, it felt like there was something in her throat. She suspected it was her heart.

THROUGHOUT THE HOUR PLUS RIDE TO ANAHEIM, Olive bounced around in the back of the SUV limousine like a ping-pong ball. "Why won't you people tell me where we're going?" she pouted, glancing out one side of the vehicle before racing over to the other. Despite the red top with black polka dots and black capris Temperance had bought her to wear for the occasion, the girl was still blissfully clueless of their plans. "What's taking so long? Where's all this traffic going?"

"Have patience, *niña*," Temperance scolded with a tinkling laugh. "It won't be long until your questions are answered."

Bexley sensed Temperance was the most excited of anyone the way her eyes sparkled with each of Olive's questions. As promised, she had made all the arrangements for their stay, including an evening with Olive at the resort's spa while Bexley worked, and new luggage for Olive with two new sets of clothes and swimsuits, pajamas, a robe, and other accessories secretly packed inside. Bexley put her foot down when Temperance suggested they take a helicopter to avoid rush hour traffic. Olive didn't need to be exposed to that degree of lavishness.

Bexley continued the search for Sadie along the way, using her laptop to check jail rosters and keep in touch with Red and Summer Landry. Although Red continued to monitor Sadie's credit cards and any general internet hits on her name, they were still clueless as to where she could be. It seemed inevitable another trip to Minnesota would be in Bexley's near future. She just wasn't sure when she'd find the time.

At last the limousine pulled up in front of a grand Craftsman-style building with a dark green roof. The buzz of the intercom crackled around them. "We have arrived at your first destination of the evening, Miss Rose," the driver's smooth voice announced. "I'll meet you outside with your luggage."

"*Gracias*, Renardo," Temperance called back.

With her nose pressed to the window, Olive's eyes rounded. "We're sleeping *here*?"

"*Si*," Temperance confirmed, reaching out to squeeze the girl's shoulder. "You and I are going to enjoy a girls' night after *un especial* dinner."

Olive turned to Bexley, sweetheart lips pulled into a pout. "You're not staying with us?"

Bexley's heart sank. She really wished she could witness Olive's expression as they dined with the park's characters. "I have to work on a case, but I should be back before your bedtime." She tugged on one of Olive's braids intricately woven by Temperance. "Don't forget your manners, and do as Temperance says."

For the first time since Bexley met Olive, she

looked close to tears. "You're coming for Temperance's surprise tomorrow though, right?"

"I'll try my best," she promised as Temperance opened the door. "Have fun, Olive. There aren't many girls your age who get this kind of experience."

"Oh, I know I'm super lucky," Olive sang, grinning. "I don't think there's anyone in the world as nice as Temperance."

Taking Olive's hand, Temperance winked. "I'm the one who's lucky, *la novia*." She threw a smile in Bexley's direction. "Please do not work so hard tonight, Miss Bexley."

Bexley simply nodded as they climbed out of the limousine. She watched as the driver delivered their luggage to a bellman with Olive skipping at Temperance's side close behind.

Olive's life was about to drastically change again. Bexley worried how the girl would adjust after she'd been spoiled by Temperance.

Uma Trembly's grandparents lived in a modest, two-story stucco home twenty minutes from the resort. As the dozens of houses in the peaceful neighborhood were identical, Bexley checked the address twice before pressing the doorbell. After the second ring, a slight woman around 70-years-old with short, silver-gray hair cut in a spiked style answered the door with a friendly expression.

"Good evening, young lady." Her eyes rounded when she spotted the limousine parked at the curb, and her fingers clutched the collar of her sea green button-down featuring white anchors. "Oh goodness. Have I won something?"

"I'm afraid not." Bexley all at once felt bad for crushing the woman's dreams. "My name is Bexley Squires, ma'am. I'm a private investigator from Papaya Springs. I'm hoping to have a minute with your granddaughter. Is Uma here?"

The elderly woman's mouth hardened, and her green eyes narrowed. "That poor child has had enough of that dirty town to last a lifetime."

I know the feeling, Bexley mused. "I was told she was unfairly harassed by her friends and classmates," she said. "I promise you it's not my intention to upset her in any way. I'm merely hoping she can help me fill in some blanks on a case."

Eyes temporarily closed, the woman shook her head. "I'm sorry you came all this way, Miss Squires, but I don't think—"

"It's okay, Grams," a high voice chirped from somewhere inside. "You can let her in."

With a reluctant expression, the woman opened the door wide enough for Bexley to slip inside. "My granddaughter is going through a rough time," she whispered. "Please keep that in mind."

Nodding, Bexley followed her a few feet into a small den painted the color of sand in which the sole wall hanging consisted of a wooden cross. Uma was curled up on a maroon leather sectional with a homemade quilt and hardcover book sprawled across her lap. Cheeks plump, gray-blue eyes shadowed, honey blond hair piled in a nest on top of her head, Uma was almost unrecognizable from the pictures Red had added to Teddy's file. Without a trace of makeup she possessed a youthful innocence, appearing closer to sixteen than her true age of eighteen.

Retrieving a stainless steel pink bottle tucked in at her side, Uma met her grandmother's stern expression. "Could you please get me more water and some ice, Grams?"

"Of course, dear." Her grandmother took the bottle, throwing Bexley a look of caution before leaving the room.

"I heard you've been trying to get ahold of me,"

Uma started, briefly eyeing Bexley's Adidas slip-ons. "I don't know what I could possibly have to do with Teddy's accident."

Bexley moved over to sit on the other end of the sectional. "From what I understand, Teddy was trying to help you with something."

Pinching her rounded cupid's bow lips together, Uma shook her head several times while wrapping her arms around her middle. "I don't know what you're talking about."

"Really? Because after Teddy had his accident, his parents found a strange notebook full of names that involved you and your friends. It seemed he was keeping a tally of his grievances with all of you. Not only that, but he had a map of the school that included your locations, as well as Mr. Fred's. In fact, his class was circled in red." She leaned a little closer and took a deep breath. "Uma, they found *a gun* in his car."

Uma let out a sharp gasp. "What?"

"I need to know what happened between you and Teddy. You seem to be the link between whatever he was going through at school, and what he'd planned to do until the accident happened. This is serious business. I believe he may have intended to harm your friends."

"He wouldn't," Uma whispered with tears in her eyes.

"Well he was planning *something* unsavory, and I have good reason to believe you're at the center of it all."

Uma set the book and blanket aside before standing.

Between her light blue cropped T-shirt and faded jean shorts, her belly was swollen. Aside from the small bulge, she was otherwise in exceptional shape.

Bexley gasped. "Uma, are you—"

"Let's take this conversation out back," Uma urged, glancing toward the kitchen. "My grandparents only know a sliver of my situation. The truth would devastate them."

PART II

CHAPTER ELEVEN

PAPAYA SPRINGS, CALIFORNIA

AUGUST 20TH OF THE PRIOR YEAR

Uma Trembly couldn't wrap her head around the great start to her senior year at Papaya Springs Academy. Her parents had surprised her with a used 2 Series BMW on the first day of classes. A mere day later, Zack Lens, the hottest and richest senior, had flirted with her over lunch block. On the third day, she was selected as a student aid for her favorite teacher, Mr. Fred.

Fred Finnegan was both crazy hot and incredibly flirtatious with the popular girls. During cheerleading practice that summer, Uma and her teammates had gossiped about rumors they'd heard involving him sleeping with a senior the year before. The afternoon he asked Uma to come by to review the syllabus, she ditched last block early to touch up her hair and makeup before changing into her cheerleading uniform—the shortest skirt allowed by the academy's strict policy. Her family had the least amount of money of any of her friends, but she was ready to prove she was still the best looking of any girl who ever stepped foot in Papaya Springs Academy.

Her efforts were instantly rewarded the moment she stepped inside his classroom on the far end of campus. Eyes the color of melted chocolate surveyed every inch of the tight body she'd earned from a meticulous diet and vigorous exercise. When she pictured slipping her fingers through his flawless flow of luxurious brown hair as he kissed her with that dreamy mouth, she warmed from head to toe.

"Go Panthers," he rumbled in his deep, sexy voice.

Giggling, Uma tossed her blond curls over one shoulder and twisted a finger through one of the locks. "I better see you in the stands tonight, Mr. Fred. We need more of that school spirit at our first home game."

His thick lips broke out in a grin. "I wouldn't

miss it for anything." He moved away from the chair behind his desk and patted its backside. "Come have a seat, Uma. We'll go over everything you need to know on my laptop."

She sashayed over to him, knowing he was tracking her every move. Before she sat she purposely bumped into him, brushing her chest over his bare arm. "Oops, sorry."

"No problem." His warm, spicy cologne tickled her nose as he leaned over her shoulder to wake his laptop. "This should be a piece of cake for you, considering your GPA and your portfolio. Your grade in my Comp class last year was the highest of anyone. Have you considered either becoming a writer or pursing a masters in English?"

"I really don't know what I'm going to do next year," she admitted. "I mean…I wouldn't know the first thing about writing a whole book. Don't you have to be, like, really creative and whatever?"

"There are all different kinds of writing careers. Some are more technical." His index finger jabbed at the keyboard, but the screen didn't respond. "Hold on, it does this sometimes." Next thing she knew, his arms were sandwiched around her as he typed with both hands. Her pulse raced when his rough cheek lightly brushed hers as he leaned in closer. "Don't worry about your future, Uma. You're a smart, beautiful young lady with a lot of potential. Once we get to know each other a little better, I'm sure I'll be able to help you figure things out."

Her stomach flipped excitedly.

AFTER THE GAME THAT NIGHT, EVERYONE WAS IN high spirits. The PS Panthers had beat their L.A. rivals by one touchdown in the last quarter. In the hallway leading to the locker rooms, a sweaty Zack Lens pulled Uma aside to flirt once again, telling her she better not miss the after-party on the beach. He was so good looking in his football uniform, dark hair tousled every which way, that she'd blushed during their entire conversation. She couldn't wait for the party as she sensed he intended to do far more than flirt.

As the cheerleading team's captain, she was last to change out of her uniform and close up the locker room. When she pulled the locked door shut, she spun around and let out a squeal. A dark figure lurked in the hallway.

With a nervous giggle, she held a hand over her heart. "Oh my god! You scared me half to death!"

"You were a star on that field tonight, Uma," Mr. Fred told her, moving in closer. "I wanted to let you know just how much I enjoyed watching you cheer."

CHAPTER TWELVE

PAPAYA SPRINGS, CALIFORNIA

FEBRUARY 10TH

Uma waited outside the doorway of Mr. Fred's classroom as his last students of the day vacated. He was still as handsome as he'd been when she'd first come to him as a student aid, but her perception of him had changed. With every female student he waved along or threw a wink to, her insides raged with jealousy. She was starting to wonder if he really thought she was as special as he made her believe, or if she was just like every other high school girl he deemed worthy of flirtation. And then there were the ugly rumors…ones that had made her green with envy. She was starting to wonder if they could be true.

Once the room had emptied, she rushed at him with an army of agitated butterflies charging through her stomach. "I need to talk to you."

Glancing between her and the doorway, he gritted his teeth. "I thought I told you we can't be seen together outside of class."

The bitterness in his tone made her flinch, but she quickly recovered. "Why does it matter when I'm still *your student aid*?" she snapped. "Besides, it's really important."

He snagged her arm, dragging her back toward the exit. "I'll call you as soon as I've left campus."

"I'd rather talk to you in person," she pouted, trying to keep her lips from trembling. His grip hurt, and she didn't understand why he was being so mean. "Please?"

"Fine," he bit out. "I'll meet you at Tristan's place around eight."

"Can't I just come over to your house?" She detested the whine in her voice, but she was beyond frustrated. She hated the way he made her come to his buddy's apartment whenever he was out of town so they wouldn't be seen together. "I'm tired of being treated like your dirty little secret."

With a deep huff, Mr. Fred released her to fold

his arms across his chest. "Justina moved in with me last weekend."

Uma recoiled as if slapped. She'd first learned he was seeing the college sophomore on the side a few months back when a naked selfie appeared on Mr. Fred's unlocked cell phone screen. "You promised you weren't going to see her anymore!" Uma cried. "You said you loved me and *only* me!"

"Keep your voice down," he growled, nudging her through the door's threshold. "We'll talk about this *later.*" The sound of the door slamming in her face echoed down the empty hallway.

WHEN SHE STEPPED INTO TRISTAN'S APARTMENT that night, she immediately recognized the signs that Mr. Fred was already drunk. The mossy scent of whiskey rolled off him, and his eyes were glazed over. He wore nothing more than a pair of low-slung athletic shorts, and his dark hair tumbled in a messy wave to one side. He looked as if he'd just finished a round of aggressive boxing.

"Sorry about earlier, baby," he slurred, running a fingertip along her bare shoulder. He moved in closer, trapping her in his arms. "You know how much trouble I could get in if someone found out about us, right?" His soft lips left a trail of kisses along her jaw. "It'd kill me if I couldn't see you again. I love you so damn much, Uma."

For a brief moment, her heart softened. "If that's true, then why are you still with Justina?"

"I'll break up with her…maybe after Valentine's Day…I promise." He nuzzled her neck and began swaying to a silent tune. "You're truly the only one I love, Uma. Only you, baby. One day we'll get married…start a family."

When he leaned away to drink from the highball glass in his hand, Uma felt a rush of unease. For the first time since the night of the academy's victory over the L.A. team, when he'd brought her back to that same apartment, she hated the way his muscles flexed throughout his tanned chest and thick arms. She hated the way he eyed her with a predatory look, expecting her to do everything he commanded. She hated that he was only nice to her when they were alone. She hated that he was always drunk when they were alone.

"I'm pregnant," she blurted.

"You're *what?*" he roared. He nudged her backwards and turned to slam the glass onto the kitchen island. "Uma, that isn't funny!"

"I took two tests last night. There's no question it's yours." When she remembered how she'd blown Zack off to be with Mr. Fred that first fateful night, she wanted to curl into a ball and cry herself to sleep. "I haven't slept with anyone else since the first time we hooked up."

With a dangerous look in his eye, he took two strides back to her. "Then you have to fix it."

"*Fix* it?" she repeated. "I'm not killing my unborn baby, Fred."

"*Your* baby?" he snarled. "I get a say in what happens to *my* child!"

"I'm not terminating this pregnancy," she repeated in a calm, steady voice. "If you try to make me, I'll tell everyone you're the father."

He lifted his drink, laughing over the rim. "Like anyone would believe you over me. You're just a loose school girl with a ridiculous crush."

Anger heated her limbs. She never dreamed he'd react to the situation with so much hatred. A mere month prior he'd confessed his love and promised they'd be together forever.

"There are tests to prove it!" she yelled. "And besides, I've been hearing nasty rumors about you! Everyone is saying you're sleeping with *several* girls at the academy! If that's true, I'll convince them to come forward with me! Your pathetic ass won't be allowed near any kind of school ever again!"

He snagged her wrist in a painful grip. "You're eighteen now. It's perfectly legal."

"I wasn't eighteen at the time this baby was conceived." Suddenly panicked, she attempted to wiggle away. She hadn't seen that side of him before. How bad would he hurt her? "How do you think *the academy* would react to a teacher sleeping with minor students?"

Yanking her wrist inward, he brought her taut against his bare chest. "Don't play a game that you can't win, little girl. I'll bury you alive."

She finally broke free and fled to the parking lot, her face soaked with tears. Starting a relationship with Mr. Fred had been the biggest mistake of her life.

CHAPTER THIRTEEN

PAPAYA SPRINGS, CALIFORNIA

FEBRUARY 11TH

The next day at the academy, Uma started asking around, hoping to uncover more details on who else Mr. Fred might be sleeping with. Over lunch block, when she got the cold shoulder from Zack Lens and the crew of friends they had in common, she feared the gossip of Mr. Fred's affairs included her. Lexie, her closest friend since the 8th grade, wouldn't even glance her way.

Sickness washed over her when she stepped into Mr. Fred's classroom for AP English and he quickly cast her a sinister look. She wasn't sure if the baby was making her sick, she was simply afraid of what Mr. Fred would do after his threats, or if it was because she was terrified by the sudden reality that she'd have to deal with the pregnancy on her own. Her parents would be livid once she was forced to drop out of college to raise a child.

From the next seat over, Teddy Renner, the most annoying person she knew, repeatedly flicked the back of her bicep with a pen. She despised Mr. Fred for teaming them up on their upcoming Shakespeare project. As if trying to translate the old dude's weird playwright about a couple of prepubescent kids having premarital sex hadn't been painful enough.

"What's going on with you, Trembly?" Teddy asked. "You look like you're gonna hurl."

"None of your damn business," she snapped, jerking out of his reach.

"If you're worried about the rumor going around, don't waste your time. No one believes that shit."

Her heart galloped as she turned to face him. "*What* rumors?" she spat.

From the front of the classroom, Mr. Fred cleared his throat. "Is there something wrong, Ms. Trembly?"

If it was possible to die of embarrassment, Uma would've been DOA the moment everyone turned to gawk at them. Tears of humiliation burned behind Uma's eyes as she slowly shook her head.

Mr. Fred held Teddy's gaze and chuckled. "Your time wasted on possible romance would be better spent on decoding the plight of Romeo and Juliet, Mr. Renner."

The entire class responded with loud laughter. Uma slumped in her desk, becoming more and more mortified with every cocky look Mr. Fred threw out through the remainder of the block. It seemed he was already playing whatever manipulative game he'd schemed in order to shun her from her classmates.

When the end of the torturous block finally came around, she snagged her bag off the floor and blindly ran for the exit. She was rounding the entrance to the girl's bathroom in the quietest wing of campus when she heard Teddy calling her name.

"That guy's a dick," he told her. "Don't let him get to you."

She spun around. "What rumor were you talking about?"

"You mean you haven't heard?" Adjusting his squared stance, he glanced over his shoulder before leaning in. "Everyone is saying you…ah…let an entire group of frat guys from PSC have their way with you last weekend. Someone sent my bitch of a sister a picture of you…in one of the frat houses with a label that said they'd all had their turn. Everyone has seen it by now. You're…wearing your cheer skirt, and…uh…nothing else."

With a sudden memory of Mr. Fred convincing her to pose topless, she covered her face with her hands. The guest room in Tristan's apartment was set up with a bunkbed so Tristan's younger twin brothers had a place to stay when they came to visit. It would've looked close to the frat house bedrooms she'd seen at parties.

"Oh god, it's really happening," she muttered to herself. Her mind raced as she wondered what other damaging evidence Mr. Fred could dig up next. "He'll ruin my reputation—no one will believe me when I say he's the father." Her stomach twisted as tears tumbled down her cheeks. "What am I going to do?"

A gentle hand touched her shoulder. "You're pregnant?" Teddy asked in a soft voice.

Gasping, she sprung away from him. In her grief, she'd forgotten she wasn't alone. "No, I mean—"

"Who's the father?" Teddy demanded, frowning. His expression hardened. *"Mr. Fred?"*

Panic rose in her throat. "What? No! Why would you think that?"

"I pick up on vibes better than most people. You haven't been acting yourself the past couple of days. And he was intentionally mean to you today. I saw him sneaking dirty looks in your direction when he thought no one was watching."

When she saw the conviction in his eyes, she clutched his upper arm. "You better not tell a single person what you *think* you know, Teddy Renner. Understand me? He told me he'll deny we were ever together. Even if I took a paternity test, my parents—*everyone*—would say it's my fault, that I somehow seduced him. Especially now…" She released him to bury her face in her hands before another sob could slip out. "Oh my god, I'm so stupid!"

"He's in a position of power, Uma," Teddy insisted. "It's an ethical violation. Having an affair with minor students is statutory rape. Even if you're eighteen now—"

"I don't care about any of that!" she roared. "He said he loved me!"

"He's *a sexual deviant* who shouldn't be allowed anywhere near high school girls!"

With the sound of high heels clicking against

the floor somewhere nearby, Uma whirled around and headed back toward the bathroom. She paused, glancing at Teddy over her shoulder. "Please don't repeat a word of this to anyone. What they're saying about me is already bad enough."

CHAPTER FOURTEEN

PAPAYA SPRINGS, CALIFORNIA

MAY 4TH

The cruel stories and name calling began to die down a few weeks after Uma's "frat house scandal," replaced by new gossip about a different girl. Mr. Fred kept his distance, and treated her cordially when they were forced to interact in class. Her friends still gave her the cold shoulder, however, and she had yet to tell her parents about the pregnancy. She hid her growing belly with baggy shirts.

Teddy Renner refused to back down after discovering her secret. He'd become as pesky as a gnat, constantly buzzing in her ear, pressuring her to do something in order to stop Mr. Fred. She was forced to find new routes to each of her classes to avoid his confrontations, but there was no getting out of their seating assignment in Mr. Fred's class.

With only a month remaining before summer break, Teddy cornered her in the hallway just minutes before their class with Mr. Fred. "We need to talk, Uma. It's really important."

"Are you crazy?" she spat, dragging him around the corner. She waited to make sure no one was coming, before leaning in to whisper, "You have to stop harassing me like this! They'll start circulating nasty rumors about me all over again!"

"Then meet me at Break-fast Surf Club after cheerleading practice," he insisted. "It's out of the way, and no one that goes here would be caught dead in that area of town. Trust me, you're going to wanna hear what I have to say."

With a huff, she reluctantly agreed.

"I've been following Mr. Fred for the past two months," Teddy told her.

Uma's stomach roiled. She glanced around the 80s themed diner, terrified someone was listening in on their conversation even though they were the only patrons at 4:30 on a Tuesday. She eyed Teddy hard. "Are you *crazy*?"

"Maybe. I have a touch of OCD and some other undiagnosed issues. I had to know if he's manipulating any other girls like he did with you. I put all my observations into a notebook, and came up with a conclusion."

She ran her bottom lip between her teeth. She still hated the idea of Mr. Fred being with other girls, but curiosity won. "What?"

"He's been going through a rotation of our classmates. *Your friends,* Uma. Lexie, Sarah, Madison, Ava, Lily…as far as I can tell without actually watching them through the window, he's sleeping with all of them."

"Oh my god." All her closest friends—including *Lexie*—were sleeping with Mr. Fred too? All at once feeling ill, Uma gripped her stomach. "Are you sure?"

"He meets them at one of the skyscraper apartments downtown on Wall Street, then later goes home to his girlfriend at his house. I can't think of any other reason why he'd want that kind of secrecy."

The restaurant tilted beneath her. "That's his friend's place. That's where we always met." The betrayal of Mr. Fred and her friends sliced deep. "Oh god…you're right. If he's taking them there, it can only mean one thing."

"There's no way of saying this without hurting your feelings, but there's a definite pattern. He goes after the most popular girls with the bitchiest attitudes. It's probably nothing more than a game to him. Maybe he's going after that type to prove something…I don't know. But someone needs to stop that sick son of a bitch, or he'll just keep doing it as long as he's a teacher."

Uma curled into herself on the bench, wrapping her arms around her knees. She'd been a fool for believing a word he'd ever uttered. "You don't have any actual proof."

"I don't need proof." His expression turned stone cold as he placed the palms of his hands on the table. "I looked into her eyes when I asked her if she had sex with him, and I saw the truth."

"Who are you talking about?"

"Doesn't matter. She was a victim just as much as you are." His eyes darted to the window overlooking the beach. "I lost my shit once I knew that creep had touched her. She made me promise I wouldn't say anything to anyone, but I can't just sit back—"

"You can't, Teddy." She gripped one of his hands over the table, making him look at her. "Whoever she is, her life would be ruined. It was *her choice* to give him her body. It should be *her choice* whether or not she wants to tell anyone. If you care about this girl, you'll keep her secret."

"That's really how you still see it?" He flipped his hand around, looping his fingers through hers. "Uma, you're all his *victims*. You were made to believe it's okay to sleep with a teacher. Maybe if you talked to some kind of crisis counselor, they'd help you feel comfortable enough to testify—"

"No!" She jerked her hand away from his and slid from the booth. "I'm sorry about whoever it is you're protecting, and I appreciate your concern, but if you think I'm going to testify against him, you truly are crazy. As much as I hate him for what he did to me, I still don't want him to go to jail." All at once feeling protective of her unborn child, she rested a hand over her belly. "Let it go, Teddy. *Please*."

As she walked away from him, she had a dreadful feeling he wouldn't stop.

PART III

CHAPTER FIFTEEN

ANAHEIM, CALIFORNIA

MAY 25TH

Bexley's chest filled with empathy as tears tumbled down Uma's cheeks. Obviously, Teddy was right. All those girls had been manipulated by Mr. Fred—*groomed* into thinking it was okay to sleep with him. Bexley didn't intend to let him get by with it. "You don't have any idea who Teddy was talking about?" she asked. "Do you think maybe he'd been dating one of the girls listed in his notebook?"

"As far as I know, he never dated *anyone* at the Academy. That's just not his thing. He cared more about his grades." Wiping at her face, Uma let out a long sigh. "I don't believe Teddy would've hurt any of us. He felt bad for what had happened. I think he intended to go after Mr. Fred that day to make him admit what he was doing."

Bexley sucked in a long, calming breath. Once she knew all the factors driving Teddy's mindset, she had to agree. Whomever's eyes he'd talked about looking into was obviously someone he cared deeply for, and discovering she had been a victim was likely what drove him over the edge. "You're probably right. But there are better, far less violent and combative ways to get a confession out of Mr. Fred." She tilted her head at Uma. "Would you be willing to meet with him again, wearing a wire? You could tell him you wanted to apologize for everything, and make him a part of his child's life. I could coach you on what to say and wait nearby in case the conversation didn't go well."

Uma sat taller in the metal patio chair, eyes cast downward. "I don't know…I would have to tell my parents and my grandparents the truth. They think I'm pregnant after a random hookup at a party, and I don't know the father."

Of course Fred hadn't volunteered to take responsibility, Bexley fumed. "I don't want to pressure you into anything, Uma, but this man is a dangerous predator. He'll continue to go after other girls like you if we don't do something. Please at least consider it." She retrieved a business card from her handbag and handed it over. "In the meantime, if any of his other victims reach out to you, I want you to call me. I'm going to put a little pressure on them, see if they'll agree to speak out against Mr. Fred. They might lash out and blame you."

"They won't stand up to him," she huffed, shaking her head over and over. "He'll threaten to ruin them the way he did with me."

"Then I'll have to get a little more creative." Bexley considered the information Uma had provided. If nothing else, she could try a little old-fashioned surveillance on the apartment the way Teddy had. "One more question—do you know the last name of this friend Tristan?"

"It's Hayes. H-A-Y-E-S. I saw it on bills and stuff."

"What about an address?"

"It was on Wall Street and Second."

"This is good, Uma. You've been extremely helpful." Bexley reached out to shake the girl's hand. "Thank you for being honest with me. It took a lot of courage for you to talk about what happened. Whether or not Teddy pulls out of this,

his parents may be able to rest a little easier knowing his intentions weren't as vile as they seemed." She rose from the patio chair and slung her handbag over her shoulder. "Take care of yourself, Uma. And good luck with the baby."

As she turned away, Uma asked, "Can you do me a favor?"

Spinning back around, Bexley dipped her chin. "Sure."

"If Teddy wakes up, can you tell him I said thank you, and I'm sorry about…everything? I feel like the accident was my fault. Maybe if he hadn't been so distracted that morning—"

"I can assure you, the accident had nothing to do with you, Uma." She offered the girl a reassuring smile. "But I'll let him know you're thinking of him."

UMA'S STORY HAD TAKEN SEVERAL HOURS TO TELL, and traffic heading back toward the resort was congested due to a multi-car pile up on the freeway. By the time Bexley slipped into the suite, the room was dark and quiet. A moment after she flipped on the nearest light, a nearby door opened and

Temperance emerged in a short satin robe with a delicate pink floral print. Her long dark hair fell over her shoulders, and her face was scrubbed free of makeup. Bexley had never seen her look so beautiful.

"Is she asleep?" Bexley asked.

"*Sí.* She missed you, but we still had a lovely time," Temperance assured her. "I took lots and lots of pictures for you."

Bexley let out a long sigh. "I swear I tried to make it back earlier."

"I'm sure you did." With a kind smile, Temperance started for the full sized refrigerator to retrieve a bottle of sparkling wine. She patted the granite island top. "Come, have a drink with me, *mi amiga*. You've had a long day."

"I'm not one to turn down a bottle of wine." She sat on one of the stools while Temperance collected wine glasses and a bottle opener from the cupboards. "I know how much you dislike it when I say this, but I'm *seriously* going to owe you for all you've done. For both me *and* Olive. Keep it up and I'll have to restrain you from showing any more generosity with a court order."

Temperance let out a tinkling laugh. "Let me ask you something." She sat the wine glasses on the island between them and smiled. "If I hadn't volunteered to watch Olive while you're working, where would she have spent her time?"

"She would've bounced between daycare and Cineste's place."

With a nod, Temperance worked on opening the bottle. "And had I not spent my money on this *niña* in need, where do you suppose it would've been spent?"

"The way you've been donating to charities lately? That's hard to say."

"It's my pleasure to share my wealth with you and Miss Olive. It's not talent or too much hard work that made me rich, *era estúpida* luck. Why shouldn't I share it with others?" She let out a delighted squeal when the cork gave with a loud pop, then began pouring the wine into the glasses. "Doing kind things for the people I care about gives me great joy."

"Olive certainly wasn't wrong when she said you're the nicest person in the world." Picking up a glass by the stem, Bexley met Temperance's smile. "There's something I've been meaning to tell you. It's about Olive's situation."

"*Aye Dios mío.* You found her mother?"

"No. But I haven't given up yet." With a heavy

sigh, she set the wine glass back down. "Olive isn't my niece, Temperance. I had a test done on her hair. We're not blood relatives."

"Oh no." Temperance's lips trembled and her eyes widened. "What does that mean for Ms. Olive?"

"After seeing the condition of her last home, it's likely child services won't let her return to her mom even if we were to locate her. I felt an obligation to take her on when I thought she may have been my niece. Now that I know the truth, it doesn't seem fair to make her continue to live this way. I simply don't have the kind of lifestyle that allows for a child. She deserves a permanent home with a family who will love her and be around to make sure all her needs are met."

Lips parted, Temperance flushed. "I can be her *familia*! I can tell the courts I want her to live with me! She loves it there, and I already adore Miss Olive as if she were my own!"

"That's a big commitment to make after only spending a week with her," Bexley said, thoroughly shocked. "And I'm sure there are a lot of hoops you'd have to jump through before they'd approve you as her guardian. Especially since you'd be dealing with child services from two different states."

"It's no matter. I will call them tomorrow to start the process. They will see I can give her a happy, safe place to live, and they will approve me so I can give Olive the good news. You will see!" With a child-like giggle, Temperance rushed around the end of the island to embrace Bexley. "Oh, *mi amiga*, I have never been this happy!"

Bexley laughed along. "Just wait until tomorrow when we visit the happiest place on Earth!" She wasn't sure why she hadn't considered the idea before, although it was likely because she had only seen Temperance as a temporary solution. But it was easy to see Olive had already formed a tight bond with Temperance. Bexley didn't doubt child services would see it too.

Temperance backed away, eyes shining with tears. "Do you think I'd make a good *madre*?"

Cupping her friend's face in her hands, Bexley smiled. "I think you'd make an *excellent* one."

THE FOLLOWING DAY, OLIVE DRAGGED TEMPERANCE and Bexley around the theme park with the energy of a jackrabbit, dressed in the feminine pink sundress Temperance had gifted her early that morning. She had burst into tears when Temperance surprised her with a pink set of ears embroidered with her name. Olive hadn't stopped beaming once the park's sign, stretched across the sky, had come into view.

As they made their way around the property, a war of emotions waged inside Bexley. She had faith that Temperance would be approved as a guardian and follow through with caring for Olive. Still, every time they passed a teenage girl, her conscious grew heavier. How many students had been a victim of Fred Finnegan's manipulative games? Although she was technically clocked out for the weekend, she worried every minute she let Fred go free was another minute he could be spending with a minor.

As they stood waiting in a long line for a spinning ride that would undoubtedly make Bexley turn green, Olive tugged on her arm. "My other aunts are here!"

Temperance and Bexley turned to search the crowd until they spotted Kiersten and Cineste headed their way with Luke and Alex close behind. Bexley burst out laughing when she noticed they were all wearing different variations of "ears." Kiersten and Luke's were wedding themed, while Alex wore classic black ears and Cineste's included a polka dotted red bow in the center.

"Aren't the four of you *precioso*?" Temperance sang. She rushed to the gate to give each of the women a hug and kiss on their cheeks.

"Are you guys going on the ride with us?" Olive asked them.

Bexley caught Cineste's panicked look. She could practically see her sister turning green with the idea, and knew she'd struggle to find an excuse that didn't reveal her condition. Bexley squeezed Olive's shoulder. "Why don't just you and Temperance go this time? I'm not sure my stomach can handle this one anyway."

Temperance tugged on Olive's hand. "Come on, *niña*. We will meet them by the exit."

Bexley ducked out of the line, motioning to Kiersten's ears. She had to admit her friend was disgustingly cute in a vintage character t-shirt and white shorts. "I missed the memo that we're doing your stag and stagette party today," she teased. "Time to line up the chocolate milk shots and watch the characters shake their dirty tail feathers!"

Kiersten grinned and lifted her hands in an animated hug. "When in Rome."

Luke slung his arm around Kiersten's neck. "Where are *your* ears, Squires?"

She motioned to her plain white t-shirt. "I couldn't find a pair that didn't clash with my outfit." She mentally rolled her eyes when she noticed *his* t-shirt was the male character version of Kiersten's. "Can I borrow you for a minute?" She winked in Kiersten's direction. "I'll make sure he doesn't break out the single bills if we come across one of the princesses."

"We were just going to buy some of those giant pretzels at the place next door," Cineste told her sister. "If we're not at the exit for this ride, we'll be over there."

Luke practically skipped beside Bexley as they made their way around the spinning ride. "What's up?"

With her hands on her hips, she huffed. "While only a man confident in his masculinity could get by wearing those ears, I'm asking you to go into attorney mode. Could you maybe take them off for a minute?"

Laughing, he swiped them off his head and wiggled his eyebrows. "Kiersten said they make me look sexy."

"Kiersten would think you look sexy in a clown

suit," she snorted. "What would a prosecutor need in order to convict someone of statutory rape?"

"You really know how to kill a party." His expression became stern. "Are there more than three years between the parties?"

"It was between a male teacher and a female student."

"Oof. Well, teachers in California have a special 'duty of care' to their students, whether or not they're eighteen. A sexual act alone would get him fired. He'd be facing a hefty fine and possible jail time. Do you have solid proof that they were having intercourse?"

"Is a pregnancy proof enough?"

Luke answered with a half-committed nod. "It depends if the student is willing to submit to a DNA test."

Remembering Uma's reluctancy, Bexley grunted. "That's iffy."

Her phone trilled with the dark theme song Red had designated to her number.

"You're into *Star Wars* now?" Luke asked, chuckling. "Hawk isn't going to recognize you."

"When in Rome," Bexley muttered, retrieving her phone from her back pocket to accept the call. "What's up?"

"Sadie Roberts," Red answered. "In an airplane, headed to LAX from Phoenix."

Bexley grasped Luke's shoulder. "Right now?"

"As far as I can tell, she'll be boarding any minute. I got a positive hit from a picture someone posted on social media with Sadie sitting in the background. There's no question it's her, boss lady. She hasn't made any attempt to disguise her appearance."

"Why would she be coming this way?" Bexley mused, turning away from Luke when he gave her a questioning look.

"Maybe she knows you have her daughter," Red replied.

Although Sadie would never find Olive in Anaheim, it still sickened Bexley to think Sadie would be near. "How long is the flight?"

"Looks like on average it's less than an hour and a half."

With the harrowing weekend traffic in full swing, it would take a miracle for Bexley to arrive in time. Unless she had the means to faster transportation...*like a helicopter*.

"Good work, Red. I'll find a way to beat her to the airport. Send me all the information you have. I'll let you know when I get there."

"Be careful, Bex," Red urged. "You don't know what she's going through. If she feels threatened by you, she could become dangerous."

At that point, Bexley didn't care. She was finally going to have a chance to confront the woman who had hurt Olive.

CHAPTER SIXTEEN

The helicopter landed at LAX almost exactly twenty minutes before Sadie's flight. Since Bexley wasn't confident Sadie would've checked luggage and there were ample exits she could use, she'd hired Brewer's biker friends Colt and Ranger to help cover more area. She also figured Sadie would run if she saw her, so it was best to stay out of sight. Bexley sent them a physical description along with the picture Red had found of Sadie in the airport, and instructed them to tail Sadie until she was out of sight from airport security.

Less than fifteen minutes after the flight had landed, she received a text from Colt.

. . .

WE GOT HER EAST SIDE LOT C

Bexley quickly assessed which direction she needed to take from her position outside baggage claim, and ran through the crowd of travelers returning to their vehicles. It wasn't hard to spot Colt and Ranger right away as they were notably colossal, striking men who almost always wore their motorcycle club leather vests. A couple of teenage girls passing by nearly ran into one of the parking lot structure's posts while rubbernecking them.

Upon spotting Bexley, Sadie's big brown eyes rounded like saucers from where she was sandwiched between the men. It was hard to say if her expression was due to surprise or relief. In a low-cut sundress of faded red, blond hair pulled back into a loose braid, shadows under her eyes, cheap weekend bag slung over one shoulder, she appeared exhausted, as if she'd been on the run throughout the entire week.

"Oh my god! Bexley! What are you doing here? You know what? It doesn't matter. Your timing couldn't have been any better!" She elbowed Colt and Ranger, pushing her way past them. "These two *Neanderthals* are holding me against my will. Don't you carry a gun on you or something?"

"Gentlemen, thank you for your service yet again," Bexley said, handing each of them the checks she'd scribbled out in the helicopter. "I'll tip you with a case of beer next time I'm in Brewer's shop."

"Anytime," Ranger grunted, pocketing the check.

Colt frowned, shifting his weight as he pushed a lock of wavy brown hair behind his ear. "Want us to stick around awhile?"

While she didn't think Sadie was particularly dangerous, she acknowledged that it might not be the smartest thing to be alone with her quite yet. "If it'd make you feel better, you can wait on your motorcycles for a bit. I'll let you know if I need any more of your services."

"*Services?*" Sadie spat, as if she was just catching onto their exchange. "What's going on?"

"Be careful, darlin'," Colt warned. "This one has a lot of fight in her."

"What the hell?" Sadie's eyes narrowed into slits as she watched the men saunter away. "You hired these jokers to keep me here? How did you know I'd even *be here*?"

"Doesn't matter." Bexley restrained herself from strangling the woman as she approached to take the bag off Sadie's shoulders. When Sadie jerked like she was going to attempt to take it back, Bexley decided whatever possessions she had inside were enough to keep her from running away. "What I want to know is where the hell you've *been*, Sadie. You seem to have forgotten that you have a ten-year-old daughter."

"Where is Olive? Is she okay?"

"No, she's not okay! She's scared and confused because her mother abandoned her without even bothering to leave a note!"

"I had no other choice. You have to believe me, Bex." She blinked as if fighting back tears and put a little waiver in her voice, but Bexley saw past the act. "I knew once Deanne called you, Olive would be okay. I knew you wouldn't be able to turn away your niece."

Bexley let the "niece" comment slide for the time being. "How did you know Deanne called me?"

"What kind of mother do you think I am?" Sadie scoffed, turning up her top lip. "I wasn't seriously just going to abandon my daughter without some kind of plan."

Knowing she'd been conned from the beginning set Bexley's veins on fire. "I saw where the two of you were living, Sadie. It seems to me you're the kind of mother who puts her needs above her child's. Anyone with a conscience would see the conditions of that house were not fit for a little girl."

Sadie rolled her eyes. "Not everyone can afford to live on a beach in California."

A flaming surge of anger rose in Bexley's throat. "You've done your research."

"So have you." Sadie lifted her chin. "My momma told me you stopped by for a visit."

"I needed to see for myself if she was fit to care for Olive. Especially now that I know without question that I'm not really her aunt." She shuffled closer to Sadie, gritting her teeth. "I know you lied about the Captain being your father. Give me one reason why I shouldn't alert airport security and have them arrest you for fraud?"

"I'll pay you back, Bex, I swear!" Sadie cried. "Just...I need a little time! I ran into some trouble, and—"

"What kind of trouble?"

"With my employer...she's a raving psycho!" Sadie's eyes jumped around the parking lot.

"She accused me of some things, and she's not

the type to mess around! She won't stop looking until she finds me!"

Bexley briefly considered the idea. Sadie's employer *had* sounded awfully determined. "What *things*, Sadie? What is it you do for this employer?"

Sadie threw her a pitiful look. "I'm an escort, alright? I get paid good money to spend time with rich, powerful men. It's not always about sex. Most of them are just lonely because they're always on the road."

The story was easier to believe than Summer's involving office administration, so Bexley rolled with it. "What 'things' is your employer saying you did?" she repeated.

"She said I've stolen from clients, *drugged* them, and threatened to expose them."

"Considering your history, that doesn't seem too far of a stretch," Bexley huffed.

"For your information, I didn't do any of that."

"Then why would she think you did?"

"Because she's psycho!"

Scratching the back of her head, Bexley considered her options. She could call Summer, and let her deal with Sadie. Or she could call the local sheriff and tell them about the money Sadie had taken from the Captain. Maybe child services in

Minnesota would even be willing to arrest her for child abandonment, although a mere week hardly seemed like enough time to prove a real case. "Why did you come to California?"

"To find you. I was going to ask for your help in getting my employer off my back."

"How did you think I would do that?"

"By doing your thing—your investigator gig—to prove I'm innocent."

Bexley snorted through gritted teeth. "What were you going to pay me with? The Captain's money?"

"I've been saving up for a nice place for me and Olive. One where she'd have her own bedroom, and a real bed."

Worry shivered through Bexley. What if Sadie was actually able to get Olive back? "You can't just abandon your child and expect things will go back to normal."

"I didn't abandon her! I left her with you!"

"That will be for the State of Minnesota to decide. I took pictures of your house while I was there. I promise they won't approve of her returning to your care."

"Please don't do this, Bexley." Real tears welled in her eyes.

"You did this to yourself, Sadie! There were far better ways you could've handled things! Ways that didn't involve leaving Olive behind!"

"You're too smart! I know if I had asked you to watch her, you would've demanded the truth, and I don't have anyone else! You saw how my momma is!"

"Yeah, and you're not any better."

"Where is Olive? Can I at least see her?"

"She's with someone who has been caring for her all week. She can't come to meet with you today —they're busy. If you give me your number, I can arrange for something on Monday."

"Where am I supposed to go until then?"

"Use whatever money you were going to pay me to get a motel room." Bexley tossed the bag back at her. She wasn't willing to bet Sadie would stick around, but she'd be relieved if she took off again and didn't put up a fight for Olive. "As far as the situation with your employer, you're on your own."

———

FROM SOMEWHERE IN HER PITCH DARK BEDROOM, Bexley's phone buzzed with a call. She'd decided to decline Temperance's offer to bring her back to

Anaheim as she knew the cost of each helicopter ride would be outrageous. Besides, it was best to give Olive one more day of normalcy before Bexley broke the news about Sadie to everyone once they returned, and Olive's life was disrupted yet again.

She slid her phone out from beneath Brewer's empty pillow and found Sylvia Renner's name on the screen. "Mrs. Renner? What's wrong?"

"I'm sorry to bother you so early, but…my son is awake. The doctors wanted to limit the number of visitors to my husband and myself, but after we made a donation to the hospital, the administrator convinced them to make an exception. I thought maybe if you wanted to talk with him, now would be the ideal time. They aren't sure how long he'll be coherent. They think…" Her voice broke. "They think he might not be with us much longer."

Bexley flung her bed sheet aside and darted out of bed. "I'm on my way."

WITH THE AID OF BREWER'S GTO, BEXLEY arrived at the hospital in record time. Both Mr. and Mrs. Renner were waiting for her at the nurse's station right outside of Teddy's room in the ICU.

With matching red noses and swollen eyes, they each appeared overwhelmed with agony.

Sylvia sniffled as Bexley approached. "Thank you for getting here so quickly. He's not exactly making sense, but he's able to say a few words at a time. We were at least given a chance to say our goodbyes."

"We asked him about the gun," Mr. Renner added in a whisper, briefly glancing over at the nurse's station. "We asked him why he had it. He only said 'had to pay' and drifted back to sleep. We thought if there was anything you needed to ask him, maybe you could give it a try before…" he paused, wiping at his eyes with the back of his hand, "before he slips away from us for good."

Bexley's gaze skipped back and forth between the couple. "I have reason to believe Teddy's intentions that day *were* mostly noble, Mr. and Mrs. Renner. It wasn't what you first assumed. I'll fill you in on everything after I've had a chance to speak with him."

Sylvia let out a sob, and Dennis took her in his arms. "Thank you, Miss Squires," he whispered while stroking his wife's head.

Wanting to give them privacy, Bexley left them and entered their son's room. A lump rose in her throat with the sight of the dark-haired boy hooked up to life-saving machines, appearing much younger and far more innocent than 18. As hard as it had been for her to imagine having a child of her own one day, it was impossible to fathom losing one.

"Teddy?" she called out softly. "Can you hear me?"

His eyelids fluttered open, and he let out a little sound. His eyes were the same dazzling shade of cornflower blue as his sister's.

She sat down on the empty chair beside him, and took his clammy hand in hers. "Teddy, my name is Bexley Squires. I'm a private investigator. Your parents hired me to look into the reason behind the notebook they found in your room, and the gun the police found in your car. I talked to Uma, Teddy. I know everything about what happened with her and with Mr. Fred, and the other girls. She also wanted me to thank you, and let you know you're in her thoughts."

Teddy winced and his fingers fluttered inside her hand.

"You had that gun because you were going to make Mr. Fred confess. You mapped out where all his victims would be so you wouldn't have to embarrass them in front of everyone."

He gave her the slightest of nods. "Gave 'im…a…chance," he wheezed out in a deep, dry voice. "Told 'im…to…confess."

"But he wouldn't," Bexley concluded. The son of a bitch knew Teddy was onto him. "That's why you had the gun."

"Bastard…*ruined* 'er." His eyelids fluttered back shut. "*Bastard.*"

"Who else did he sleep with?" Bexley pleaded, squeezing his hand. "Who was the girl that made you so upset?"

"It was me," a soft voice answered. Bexley turned to watch Reese shuffle into the room, lips quivering, makeup streaked from tears. "He found out I slept with Mr. Fred my freshman year, and he lost his mind." She hurried past Bexley to the other side of the hospital bed and held onto her brother's arm. "Is that what you were planning to do, Teddy?" she demanded with a wrenching sob. "Were you really going to *throw your life away* because he took my virginity?"

Bexley stared at the siblings with a new sense of trepidation. She could understand why Teddy would've gone over the edge after learning his young sister was one of the teacher's victims. She would've only been fourteen or fifteen.

Still sobbing, Reese laid her head on her brother's chest. "I love you, Teddy! I'm so sorry I did this to you!"

Hardly a minute passed before there was a blip on the EKG machine at his side, and a shrill alarm sounded.

"No!" Reese cried, popping upright. She shook her brother's shoulder. "Teddy, don't leave me!"

When a team of doctors and nurses entered the room, Bexley stood and stepped aside to let them do their job.

"It's all my fault!" Reese cried. Bexley went over to her, gently leading her from the room. "It's all my fault!"

Sylvia rushed to them. "What's your fault, sweetheart?" Her eyes widened with horror when she saw the activity in the room. "What's happening?"

Reese broke free from beneath Bexley's grip and ran down the hallway.

"You better go after her," Bexley told Sylvia. "I'll fill you in later."

CHAPTER SEVENTEEN

As the sun was breaching the horizon, Bexley parked in her driveway. The death of Teddy Renner had hit her hard. Although she knew there was nothing she could've done to save him, she wished she could've at least told him Fred Finnegan was behind bars before he'd died. She'd stayed with the family for several hours afterwards, filling Mr. and Mrs. Renner in on the facts while Reese was taken home by a family friend.

The Renners were devastated by what had happened to their daughter, and had insisted on reporting Mr. Fred to the authorities immediately. Bexley pleaded with them to give her one more day. She hoped at the very least she could convince Uma and Lexie to report him as well, making it a stronger case when it came time for the prosecution stage.

She planned to shower and change into her "uniform" of blue jeans and a blazer before going to meet with Lexie. But when she killed the engine, she was hit with an emotional riptide and couldn't muster the energy to move. Between her sister and Olive's situations, Sadie's appearance, and now Teddy, she was mentally drained. She hated that she had to leave Temperance, Olive, and her friends behind at the park, no matter how ridiculous they'd looked in those ears.

She craved the comfort of Brewer's strong arms around her more than ever. As much as she wanted to text him, she worried he'd only scold her for working too hard rather than empathizing with her situation. She tried to convince herself to keep it together because it wouldn't be much longer before he'd return. But when she rested her forehead on his GTO's steering wheel, big fat tears began to splash onto her lap.

What if they didn't let Brewer out early, and she had to make it through several more months without him?

What if she had spent the last year of her life chasing the wrong career?

What if she didn't have the perseverance to be a successful private investigator?

What if J.J. only encouraged her out of the goodness of his heart?

He wouldn't have trusted you with his business if that were true, she told herself.

Or maybe he's just a crazy old man who wanted to spend the remainder of his life fishing, and you refused to see the truth, another part of her conscience reasoned.

The sound of an enthusiastic bark jarred her from her self-pity party. She turned to see Cap rocketing across the sand in her direction. She didn't realize how much she had missed her furry little buddy until his warm brown eyes came into view and his tail began to wag.

"Hey, my sweet boy!" she yelled, racing out to greet him. Part of her hated that he no longer jumped and licked her face, but she was glad to see him regardless. She squatted to scratch behind his ears, allowing his long pink tongue to lap at her wet face. He was sporting a brand new US flag handkerchief around his neck. "*Who's my stylish, handsome boy?*"

"I thought that was your flashy car," Twila said, moving in behind Cap. As always, the older woman was a blur of colors and patterns, gray hair arranged in complicated buns on either side of her head. The sight of her kind smile warmed Bexley's chest. "Cap and I were just out for our morning walk when I saw headlights…figured I better come check it out. Seemed a little bit early for you to be returning home."

"In the future I'd rather you didn't investigate on your own like that, in the near-dark." Bexley stood to give the woman a scolding look. "I have a lot of enemies, Twila. I'd never forgive myself if you got caught in the middle of something ugly."

"Seems to me you have enough good friends that you shouldn't worry about anyone else," the woman scolded right back. "Anyway, I wouldn't normally stick my nose where it doesn't belong. Just thought with you being gone for the weekend, I'd look into it." Studying Bexley's face, she tilted her head and flattened her smile. "Everything alright, sweetheart? You look downright exhausted. I know that's not something you're supposed to say to a woman, but seems to me you could use some cheering up."

"It's been a long week," Bexley admitted, trying to control the waiver in her voice. "Scratch that… it's been a long few *months*."

"I'd miss that handsome man of yours too." She

wiggled her eyebrows and laughed. "Don't worry, dear. He'll return to you before you know it."

"Did someone tell you he's getting home early? Is that why Cap is cosplaying as Captain America?"

Twila tapped her temple, smirking. "Just intuition."

Bexley laughed. "I could use a little of that. It would sure make my life a lot easier."

"I have a feeling you have more than enough, or you wouldn't be able to solve so many mysteries. How about I feed you breakfast to put some meat on your bones along with some pleasant company instead? Clean up, then come by to join me for breakfast. I was just about to prepare myself some eggs Benedict and cut up some fresh fruit from the farmer's market. I even grabbed some delightful hazelnut coffee from the corner cafe on my way back." Twila cupped her mouth and whispered, "We can add a little shot of whiskey to it."

A smile slid over Bexley's lips. "I'm starting to think you were sent by an angel."

"Perhaps the kind with a tail and horns." Twila winked, then called to Cap. "Let's go, boy. You'll see your momma again when she's all fresh for the day."

Bexley watched them skip away, still convinced

Brewer had sent the sainted woman to look out for her.

On her way to meet with Lexie at the same location on the beach as before, Bexley received another call from Sylvia Renner.

"Reese is missing!" Sylvia's anguished voice rang through the SUV's speakers. "She said she was going to lay down for awhile, but that was over an hour ago and now her room is empty. After the conversation we had with her about Mr. Finnegan, I'm afraid she ran away. She thinks Teddy wouldn't have been in the accident if he hadn't been so upset about their affair. I'm worried she'll do something...drastic." Her voice thickened with tears. "I wanted to call the police, but Dennis said the police normally don't care about a teenager unless they've been gone for a lot longer. She's upset about Teddy, and the fact that we now know what she'd gone through with her teacher. Will you please help us find her?"

"I'll do everything in my power." Bexley swung into the nearest parking lot and started to turn her vehicle around. "Have you tried checking with her friends?"

"The ones I'm friends with online claim they haven't heard from her. My sister is attempting to contact the others through their parents."

"Does she have access to a car?"

"All of our cars are accounted for."

"Does she normally have any cash on hand? Credit cards?"

"She might have a little cash, but not usually enough for any big purchases. Maybe a few tens or twenties." Sylvia let out a stuttering sigh. "She normally uses the platinum credit card we opened under her name."

"Log into your account, and see if there has been any activity. Then call the credit card company, and ask them to alert you the second she tries using it. What about ride apps? Do you share accounts, or does she have her own?"

"She uses ours."

"Log in and track those too. Let me know if you come up with anything useful. I'm going to canvas your neighborhood and the usual hangouts for the Academy students." It wasn't really where she intended to go, but she didn't want to upset the distressed mother any more.

"I can't lose another child, Miss Squires," Sylvia whimpered. "I would break."

The anguish in her voice caused Bexley's heart to plummet. "We'll find her, Mrs. Renner."

She ended the call and dialed a number she had considered removing from her contact list a few months prior. To her surprise, Grayson Rivers answered on the third ring.

"Bex? It's been awhile." Her ex-boyfriend's voice was low and cautious.

"I need to ask you a personal favor, Gray. I don't have time to explain the entire story to a dispatcher, and I don't exactly have a lot of other allies on the force except for Deputy Danks, and he's on vacation. This is urgent. I need a patrol car to meet me at the apartment skyscraper downtown on Wall Street and Second. I have a strong reason to believe a distraught sixteen-year-old girl intends to harm Fred Finnegan. The apartment he's using is rented by a buddy named Tristan Hayes, H-A-Y-E-S. I don't know the exact unit number."

"Are we talking about the same Fred we went to PSH with?"

"Yeah, and he's still having sex with high school girls."

"Wh—"

"There will be charges filed against him after this is said and done. Just please, send an armed officer immediately."

"I'm five minutes out. I'll meet you there."

As he ended the call, she cringed a little. She knew she was taking a chance by calling him, and that he would possibly volunteer to meet her instead of sending someone. But she was willing to take that chance as long as Grayson could remain civil and give the friendship thing real effort.

She was also taking a chance by guessing Reese would ask Fred to meet her at the apartment rather than going after him at his home, but she doubted Reese knew where he lived.

The SUV didn't have as much get-up-and-go as the GTO, but she managed to shave several minutes off by blowing through yellow stop lights and driving a dozen miles over the posted limit. When she rolled up to the glass skyscraper, Grayson was already leaning on the trunk of his work car, waiting. As she parked behind him, she couldn't deny there was a space in her heart that still fluttered with the sight of her handsome ex. He hadn't changed much since their breakup, except for the short beard he'd grown to match his thick dark eyebrows and neatly groomed hair.

"Dispatch said Tristan Hayes is in twenty-twelve," he told her as she stepped out onto the street. "Who's this girl we're looking for?"

"Her name is Reese Renner," Bexley said. "She's approximately five-seven with platinum blond hair, blue eyes, slim athletic build. It's likely she met Fred here several times."

Grayson's eyes seemed to go everywhere but on her as he scratched his bearded chin. "Any relation to the Renner kid who was in that bad accident with a gun in his possession?"

"She's Teddy's sister, and he died this morning. We have good reason to believe at the time of his accident he was on his way to confront Fred Finnegan about all the students he was sleeping with, including Reese. She was exceptionally upset that her brother died, blames herself for the circumstances. I've created a fairly friendly acquaintance with her. She might respond best to my direction."

Nodding, Grayson motioned to the building. "Let's head up there."

Inside the lobby entrance of sparkling glass walls and polished white granite floors, Grayson used his badge to get past the doorman and ask for directions to Tristan's unit. The elevator ride up to the twentieth floor started with several seconds of uncomfortable silence before Grayson turned to face her. "How many of Fred's students have come forward?"

"Only two so far," she admitted. "But one is pregnant with his child, and I have a fairly accurate source that lists close to a dozen more girls who attended PS Academy."

Grayson shook his head. "Christ. I always knew the guy was an asshole," he muttered, scratching his beard. "This takes it to a whole different level."

"He needs to be locked away from young girls. I just hope we can come up with enough evidence to do a proper job."

"Do you have your license to carry yet?" he asked, glancing at her hips.

She let out a hard sigh, knowing he'd be disappointed with her answer. "I don't know that I'll ever get comfortable enough to handle a handgun."

A tick of irritation crossed his jaw. "Then stay right behind me until I know the situation is secure." He threw her a frown. "*Please*, Bex. I know you can handle yourself, but you're still a civilian. Let me do my job."

"Okay," she agreed with some reluctance.

The second the elevator doors parted, Grayson

sprang out and rushed several dozen feet to unit 2012 with his service weapon drawn. "Fred Finnegan?" he called out in an authoritative voice. "It's Detective Grayson Rivers with the Papaya Springs PD! I'm here to perform a welfare check!"

After several heartbeats of silence passed, the startling cry of a girl came from inside.

Grayson and Bexley exchanged a worried look.

"I'm coming inside!" Grayson hollered. He kicked the door with his lace-up shoes several times. It gave way in a mess of shards around the handle, then he shouldered his way inside. Bexley followed close behind as instructed, watching his feet as he moved across a pristine Brazilian walnut floor.

"Do you have a weapon on your person?" Grayson demanded of Fred.

"No, and I don't know what's going on!" she heard Fred declare. "She just showed up, acting all crazy!" When peering around Grayson, Bexley found Fred standing near an open set of French doors, hands held up at his sides, wearing only a pair of boxer briefs. "Please do something before she hurts herself!"

Bexley's pulse raced with every footstep as she moved away from Grayson and started for the warm breeze coming from the open doors. Her feet moved beneath her slow and sluggish, as if fighting against quicksand. Before her brain could register the sight before her, her stomach threatened to heave.

Wearing only a pink bra and lacy white underwear, Reese stood on the steel beam lining the balcony with her back facing the ocean, face wet with tears. "If he doesn't admit what he did, I swear to God I'll jump!"

CHAPTER EIGHTEEN

Bexley held up a trembling hand between herself and the overwrought teenager. "Come down from there. Please, Reese. This is not the way to do this. Your parents are so worried. It would destroy them if they lost you too."

"Teddy wouldn't be dead if *he* hadn't convinced me what we were doing was okay!" Reese stabbed a finger in Fred's direction. "I won't let him get away with it!"

"Teddy died because an old woman was confused, Reese," Bexley disagreed in a gentle voice. "She was going the wrong way."

Reese squeezed her eyes shut and shook her head repeatedly. "He wouldn't have left for school so early that day if he hadn't planned to confront Mr. Fred!"

Fred grunted from right behind Bexley. "Confront me about *what*?"

"*Shut up, Fred!*" Bexley roared, spinning around to confront him. "This is not the time to play dumb! I spoke to Uma Trembly! I know about the baby! Fess up to what you did so we can get her down from there!"

Fred's mouth clamped shut and his eyes hardened.

In the next second, Grayson used one hand to twist Fred's arm behind his back while producing a pair of hand cuffs in the other. "Fred Finnegan, you are under arrest for lewd acts with a minor child—"

"This is outrageous!" Fred snarled as Grayson locked the cuffs into place. "What proof do you have other than this lunatic's word? I want my lawyer!"

Grayson started in on the Miranda rights as Fred continued to voice his protest. Bexley sensed Grayson wasn't exactly following protocol, and merely wanted to do something to coax Reese down.

"It's over," Bexley told Reese, sliding in a little closer with open arms. "Please, come down now."

Reese curled her bare toes down around the ledge as if locking herself in place and continued to cry. "I wanna hear him say it! Make him say it out loud!"

Bexley turned to meet Fred's glare. "Do it, goddammit!"

He shook his head, laughing. "I'm not an idiot! This is entrapment!"

"It's called being a decent human being and saving a young girl's life!" Bexley snapped back. "Prove that you're not a total monster! Do it, Fred!"

His upper lip curled, and his entire body jiggled. "I had *consensual* sex with her."

"And not just with me!" Reese prodded. "There were others! Maddie, Kendall, Lily, Lexie—"

"I banged all of them! I had sex with the entire goddamned female population at the Academy! They all wanted it!" Fred released a dry laugh while eyeing Reese with malice. "I hope that makes you happy, you little bit—"

Bexley swung at Fred's face the way Brewer had coached her before he'd left, tucking her thumb below her first and second knuckle while keeping her arm level with her shoulders. Her fist connected with his nose, spraying blood across his mouth.

"Shit!" Fred cried, buckling over in pain. "I think you broke my nose!"

Grayson fought to stifle a chuckle behind him.

Bexley shook her stinging hand. "I've wanted to do that ever since you tripped Kiersten Douglas in the junior hallway."

"You're Bexley *Ferguson*!" Fred realized, wide-eyed. "You're the loser who—"

"Better get you out of here before she cold-cocks you the next time," Grayson interrupted, excessively yanking on the handcuffs and making Fred grunt with pain.

"Are you going to clean me up?" Fred asked as they walked away.

"I'll give you a Band-Aid in the car," Grayson answered.

"That was *awesome*!" Reese burst into tears. "I wish someone had caught that on video!"

"Come on," Bexley pleaded, opening her arms to the girl one more time. "I'll take you back to your parents."

After Reese half-dropped down into Bexley's embrace, Bexley cried too.

Sylvia Renner stood outside the police station's interrogation room, daintily dabbing around her wet eyes with a sterile white handkerchief. "I don't know how to thank you, Miss Squires. You set our hearts at ease over our Teddy, and saved our baby girl. Whatever you bill us won't ever be enough for all you've done."

Bexley watched Reese embrace her father in the hallway behind them. "She's a good kid. It was my pleasure."

"What will happen to that dreadful teacher now?"

"I'm afraid there's a long process ahead," Bexley admitted. "The interview with the police was only the beginning. Courts tend to drag these things out. She might not have to testify against him at all, or she might have to testify a whole year from now. Hopefully all of his other victims will come forward now so the prosecutors have a strong case. Either way, I can't imagine he'll be allowed to step foot on any school campus ever again."

Reese and her father approached them with tired smiles.

Dennis offered a hand to Bexley. "I underestimated your capabilities the first time we met, Miss

Squires. It was sexist, and outright rude. I'd like to apologize for that."

"No harm, no foul," she said, shaking his hand. "And please, call me Bexley."

Reese hurtled herself at Bexley for a bear hug and cried.

"We'll give you two a minute alone," Sylvia said, laughing softly. "Reese, sweetheart, we'll be waiting in the lobby."

"Thank you for *everything*," Reese told Bexley, squeezing harder. "You really are a badass."

"Hardly—I'm terrified by rabbits and don't like guns," Bexley said with a laugh, patting the girl's back. "Promise me you'll be safe, kiddo, and listen to your parents. They really love you, and they're hurting. The three of you will need each other more than ever."

"I know, and I will," Reese replied before stepping back to wipe her face. A bright grin broke out against her lips as she glanced beyond Bexley. "That hot detective is watching us with a weird little look. Are you two…*together*?"

"Just because a man is 'hot' doesn't mean they're good for you," Bexley scolded.

Reese let out a dramatic snort. "So is he your boyfriend or what?"

"He was once upon a time, but it turned out we weren't good together." Her lips spread wide when she thought of Brewer. "I'm with someone now who loves me for who I am, and treats me as his equal. He's brave and honest…and incredibly kind. Don't ever settle until you find someone with all those qualities."

"Sounds like this guy of yours is a rare species."

"There are more like him out there, Reese. I promise. And you have plenty of time to find them. Don't rush into anything if it doesn't feel right."

"Yeah yeah. I better go." Her lips spread with a wobbly smile. "I'm sure my parents are eager to take me home." She threw a casual wave beyond Bexley—to where Grayson must've been standing—before turning to head toward the lobby.

With a sigh of relief, Bexley watched her for a minute before reluctantly starting toward where Grayson stood farther down the hallway, hands in his dress pants' pockets, leaning against the wall. As it was Sunday, there were only a small handful of uniformed officers in the office. Otherwise, they were alone. She didn't want to get into another fight, and she most certainly didn't want to take a stroll down memory lane when she was at her most vulnerable.

She sighed, scrubbing her hands over her face. "This has been one of the longest days of my existence. I'm going to head home to hibernate for a month or two." Although the idea was impossible, she'd take any other option to avoid the conversation she needed to have with Temperance and Olive once they returned.

"Wanna grab some wings and beer from Sandy's first?" Grayson asked.

The thought of returning to the restaurant where they'd shared many meals while they were together made her even more uneasy. Yet she wanted to thank him for disrupting his peaceful Sunday, and coming to her aid at the drop of a hat. A curious part of her wanted to know what was going on in his life, and if he was happy. They'd spent so many intimate moments together that she still cared about him.

She scrunched her nose. "I'm not really in the mood for greasy wings. How about we meet at Pollo's instead?" She wiggled her eyebrows. "My treat."

He chuckled. "Consider my arm twisted."

"In a perfect world, I would've captured you punching Finnegan on my phone," Grayson told her with a mouthful of tacos. "You would've been an internet sensation by now."

"In a perfect world, I would've knocked him out cold." Bexley sucked the sauce off of her fingers. "That jerk deserved a lot worse the way he was talking to that poor girl. She's going to need a decade of counseling to undo the damage he caused."

"She seems strong. Determined. I'm sure she'll survive and come out of it even stronger." He flashed her one of the cute grins that made her fall for him all those months ago. "She reminds me a little of another strong woman I know."

The conversation had remained casual and polite until that moment, and she was ready to get down to the nitty gritty before they parted ways. "So, what are you up to these days?" she finally asked once she'd swallowed the last of her taco. "Has anyone come along and swept you off your feet?"

"I started seeing a possible contender," he admitted with a sheepish grin. He deposited his napkin on his empty plate and leaned back in the booth. "Her name's Sofia. She works with special needs children at SH Elementary. I think you'd approve."

"Does she make you happy?"

His russet eyes danced. "Yeah...she does."

"Then I'd *definitely* approve," Bexley agreed. "You're a good man, Gray. You deserve to be with someone just as good."

He glanced away to another table. "I hear you still stop by the jail on a regular basis to visit Hawkins."

"Your staff is spying on me?" she asked with a strong surge of irritation.

His hardened gaze moved back to hers. "You still with that guy?"

"I am. We moved into a new place together... and have a rescue dog *ironically* named 'Captain'."

Grayson wiped at his face with both hands. "Christ, Bex. I'll never understand what you see in him." He removed his hands from his face and scowled. "Are you going to tell me *he* makes you happy? How? Better yet, why?"

"He makes me *ridiculously happy*—for reasons that are none of your business." She balled her hands into fists beneath the table, wincing when pain shot through the hand she'd used on Fred's face. "I don't know why you assume he's a thug, because that couldn't be any further from the truth. He's a good man, just like you. There's no reason for you to hate him. We became friends *after* I found him in that motel room with Dayna Stryker and the missing dog collar, and I didn't entertain the way he felt about me until long *after* I told you we were done."

"Good to know he had a thing for you before that," Grayson grumbled, taking the last swig from his Mexican beer.

"You know me well enough to believe I'm being truthful when I say I never cheated on you." The waitress came by with their ticket. Bexley quickly handed her a credit card and sent her back on her way with a dismissive smile. She then leaned over the table. "I want us to be friends again, Gray, without any bitter feelings. I know Kiersten invited you to their wedding. It would break her heart if there was tension between us." She sat up tall again and smiled. "Maybe once Brewer is released, the four of us could get together for dinner. I'd love to meet Sofia."

He scratched his head while glancing at the door. "I don't know."

"It would mean a lot to Kiersten if we could get along…and to me. I know I hurt you, Gray, but I still care about you. You're one of my oldest and dearest friends."

"I'll think about it." Once again, his eyes met hers. "When does he get out?"

"Not soon enough. But I'll let you know."

He turned sideways and pushed to his feet. "Thanks for lunch."

"Before you go, can I ask your advice on something?"

"What now?" he huffed with the hint of a bemused smile.

"If someone committed a crime in another state but the charges have yet to be filed, is there a way to hold them in California until the police in the other state have enough evidence for an arrest and extradition?"

"There's nothing I can think of off the top of my head," he answered, crossing his arms. "How serious is the crime?"

"It involves possible theft and drugging of victims."

He shrugged. "Any way you can convince them to stick around?"

Bexley hesitated. She hated the idea of using Olive as bait, but she hated the idea of Sadie running off with her even more. Besides, if Sadie was truly stealing from Summer Landry and a clientele of powerful men, who knows what they'd do once they found her? Keeping her in California could ensure her safety.

"I might know of a way," she decided.

"Let me know once they've been charged, and I'll help the other state arrange for the extradition." He bent to kiss the top of her head, lips lingering. "You did good with that girl today, Bex," he muttered into her hair. "Go home and enjoy a bottle of Prosecco before you hibernate. You deserve it."

As she gaped after him, surprised by the sudden act of affection, she felt a small pang of nostalgia, and a bigger rush of an emotion she couldn't identify. For a second, their friendship filled her thoughts expanding outwards like a balloon reaching for the sky and she pumped her fist with a grin. Their relationship was on the mend.

CHAPTER NINETEEN

"Stop pacing," Cineste pleaded in a whisper. "You're just going to make everyone else nervous."

Bexley stopped dead in her tracks, glancing in Temperance and Olive's direction. They cuddled together on Bexley's outdoor sofa, watching Cap and Cinderella chase the seagulls in the sand. Temperance absentmindedly stroked the girl's hair while humming. Bexley wasn't prepared for something to happen that wouldn't allow the two of them to stay together.

Bexley had been dead set against the idea of Temperance being there for the final visit, worried Sadie would recognize the reality star and add her to the list of her victims if things went a different way. But Temperance had begged to attend the meeting, wanting to meet Sadie in person, and Bexley didn't have the heart to say no. So Temperance had hired a makeup artist to transform her into the frumpy "nanny" they would claim Bexley had hired to watch over Olive. Had it not been for the seriousness of the situation, Bexley would've burst out laughing when she first saw Temperance's dull brown wig with bangs and her cheeks covered in silicon to make her appear chubby.

Because Sadie was running two and a half hours late, Bexley had missed her usual Friday visit with Brewer, and it had upset her more than she'd expected. She still felt a lingering charge from punching Fred Finnegan in the face, and wondered if she'd get the same kind of satisfaction with Sadie.

She'd been stringing Sadie along with little visits ever since Monday, waiting to receive word that felony charges had been filed and a warrant had been issued. When Summer called with the news the night before, Cineste and Bexley had celebrated with sparkling water and Prosecco along with another backyard dinner at the cottage.

"Maybe things went into motion without us knowing, and Grayson already arrested her lying ass," Cineste whispered.

With her lips set in a hard line, Bexley turned back to her sister. "Or maybe her lying ass caught onto our game, and ran for good."

Cineste pursed her lips and tilted her head back and forth like she was undecided. "There are worse ways this could end. That would just force Temperance to wait a few months before she could apply for a termination of Sadie's rights. End of story."

"I'm hungry," Olive announced in a dramatic tone. "What's taking *Sadie* so long?"

"Have patience, *bella*," Temperance said. She caught Bexley's gaze. "I'm sure your *mamá* will be here soon."

Grunting, Bexley pulled her phone from her back shorts pocket and stepped away from the patio to call Grayson, joining the dogs on the beach. "I don't know what to tell you, Gray. Every other day this week she's been here within minutes of the scheduled time. Do you think someone tipped her off about the warrant?"

"It's always possible," he answered. "Have you tried calling her?"

"Like ten times."

"Give it another half hour, then I'll put another plan into motion."

"I'm sure this isn't how you wanted to spend your Friday night."

"Sofia will have to learn my job often requires odd hours." He cleared his throat. "Hold on… there's an Uber pulling up to your house now. It's her, Bex."

Heart pounding, she swallowed and mentally psyched herself up. "Okay. I'll call you back when we're ready. I really just want Olive to say goodbye to her mom one last time."

"Try not to spook her, Bex," he reminded her before ending the call.

By the time she returned to the backyard, she heard tires pulling out of the driveway. Seconds later, Sadie meandered back to where everyone waited. "Sorry I'm s' late!" she slurred. She bent with her arms held out to Olive. "Aren't ya gonna tell yer momma hello?"

"Stay there a minute," Bexley warned, pointing in Olive's direction. "Your *momma* and I are going to have a little talk inside." The stench of alcohol stung Bexley's lungs as she escorted Sadie into the cottage and disengaged the alarm system behind them. "Where have you been? At a bar instead of here with your daughter?"

"I met someone," Sadie said with a slurred

giggle. "Someone *amazing*. Robert is a big, beautiful Marine who said he'd take good care of someone like me."

Bexley's phone buzzed with an incoming call. She quickly reached into her pocket to silence it. "What about Olive?"

"What about 'er? Isn't she safe here with you?"

"The visits with Olive are over, Sadie. You've proved you aren't fit to care for her."

A knock came from the front door. At the same time, Bexley's phone buzzed with another call. She again silenced the call as she headed for the door.

"You can't do that!" Sadie called after her. "You can't take my daughter from me!"

A tall, striking woman with iron-straight dark hair stood at the door in a tan business suit. Her eyes were as dark as coal, and her demeanor was as cold as ice. "Bexley Squires?" With a stiff smile, she crossed her arms. "Summer Landry. I wanted to personally thank you for your help."

Warning wrenched through Bexley. How did Sadie's boss know where to find her? She was stuck on that thought when the woman moved aside. A bald, beefy man with very little neck stepped in her place.

"Nicko says *no one* steals from him," the man announced.

Then he raised a pistol.

"Get down!" Bexley cried, sprinting toward Sadie.

Two gunshots rang through the air. Bexley held her breath as she crashed down on top of Sadie, head tucked beneath her arms. As she waited for the sting of a bullet, she thought of Brewer and how disappointed he'd be if she died just days before they were reunited.

"Down on the floor!" Grayson barked behind them. "Hands behind your head!"

Bexley glanced up to where Grayson stood over the shooter. He kicked the gun away and placed his foot firm against the man's lower back, several feet down from where blood poured from the shooter's shoulder. Summer was facedown on the floor beside them, hands laced behind her head.

Bexley crawled off of Sadie. She was crying, but otherwise appeared unharmed.

"Did you get hit?" Bexley asked.

Sadie shook her head with snot streaming from her nose. "I'm so sorry I brought you into this!"

"Bexley!" Cineste shrieked, running into the cottage. *"Bexley, are you okay?"*

"I'm okay," Bexley answered, scrambling to her feet.

"Keep everyone outside until the scene is secure, Cineste," Grayson ordered. "Several squad cars and an ambulance are on their way." Then his dark gaze swung over to Bexley. "Next time answer your damn phone when I call. I saw them coming up the driveway, but I couldn't get to them in time. One second later and you'd both be dead."

"I'm just lucky you have my back," Bexley replied with a shaky smile. "Again."

THE AMBULANCE HAULED THE SHOOTER AWAY, THEN Summer Landry and Sadie were transported to the PS police station in separate squad cars. Grayson stuck around, wanting to be sure the women weren't too shaken. Bexley was grateful she had taken Sadie inside, or otherwise Olive might've witnessed the shooting in real time.

"I wanna sleep at your place tonight," a sleepy Olive told Temperance, clinging to her like a koala bear. "I don't wanna be here in case those people come back."

"They're not coming back, *dulce niña*," Temperance cooed, stroking Olive's curly hair away from her weary face. "The police have taken them to jail."

"I think that's a good idea," Bexley said. "Go ahead and take her, Temp. It's past time to wash that ridiculous disguise off your face too. I'll come by in the morning and we'll discuss what happens next."

Temperance held on to Olive as she rose to her feet, then shuffled over to Bexley to kiss both of her cheeks. "Be safe, *mi amiga*."

Olive leaned in to do the same. "Goodnight, Aunt Bexley."

Tears sprung to Bexley's eyes. The poor girl should've been confused over what happened with her mother, but she was taking it all in stride. It made her wonder what Olive had already witnessed in her short lifetime. "Sweet dreams, Olive. You're safe with Temperance."

Temperance called for Cinderella to follow. Cap watched them head toward the front of the cottage with what could only be described as longing.

Cineste walked around the outdoor sofa to hug her sister. "I'm going to head out too." When they parted, she narrowed her eyes on Bexley. "Unless you want me to stay, which I totally can. Alex would be just fine on his own for a night."

Bexley decided Grayson was far enough away, deeply engaged in a phone call with the station that he wouldn't hear their conversation. "How *are* things with you and Alex? Have you told him the news him yet?"

Cineste's cheeks flushed. "I did, and he's over the moon excited. He wants to get married before the baby is born."

Jealousy struck Bexley's core. Not because of the baby, but because Cineste was planning for a real future with the man she loved. Bexley was beyond ready for something a little more solid, but that couldn't happen until Brewer was released. "I'm so happy for you, Cin. You two will be great parents. Whatever happens, you're strong enough to survive it."

"That's because I have you as a role model," Cineste told her, winking. She motioned to Grayson. "You okay being alone with him?"

"We've actually had a truce of sorts, so we'll be fine." She kissed her sister's cheek. "Go home and rest before my niece or nephew is here to create havoc on all our lives."

Cineste's eyes twinkled. "You're gonna make an awesome aunt."

Grayson ended his call, exchanging a short goodbye with Cineste on her way out. He returned to Bexley, chuckling. "She's a totally different person."

"She finally has her shit together," Bexley decided, wrapping her arms around her waist.

He studied her body language and frowned. "Want me to stay a little longer?"

"Nah, I'm good," she answered, for both of their sakes. "Cap's a pretty good watch dog, and Brewer installed a high-end security system before he left. Even a highly trained ninja would be hard pressed to sneak inside."

Grayson's eyes swept over the cottage. "It's a great place—prime location. I don't remember seeing it before."

"That's because it was a rundown shack before Brewer got his hands on it." She laughed as her eyes skipped over the restored cottage. "Believe it or not, he bought it for me as a sort of 'I'm going to jail' present. He knew I liked it, and he wanted to distract me so I wouldn't get as upset when he told me he'd taken a deal and would be starting his sentence in a couple of weeks."

"You really *are* happy," Grayson realized. "Sounds like he's good to you."

"Come have dinner with us, and you can see for yourself." She wrapped her arms around him, briefly resting her head on his chest. It felt both familiar and foreign. "Thank you, Grayson. You've saved me more times than I can count. I guess there's room for two heroes in my life. But don't get any ideas—there's only one hero I'll share my bed with."

He hugged her back, chuckling. "You're the hero in your own story, Squires. The rest of us are just your sidekicks."

Long after Grayson left, Bexley sipped on a glass of Prosecco on the couch in the backyard, nibbling on crackers with cheese while watching the ocean dance beneath the moonlight. Cap cuddled on the sofa at her side, snoring in a deep sleep. She was annoyed with herself for staying up when she was completely drained, but she was afraid once she settled in bed, her emotions would become over-whelming. She'd expected to die once she saw that shooter, and only one person flashed through her mind.

"Hello, beautiful. I'm home." With the sound of Brewer's deep voice, she yelped in a sound of surprise and delight.

She popped up from the patio sofa and blinked several times, wondering if the ridiculously handsome man in a black t-shirt and worn blue jeans was a product of her exhausted imagination. Cap ran to him, wiggling and rubbing on his legs with a whine. Laughing, Brewer squatted down to hug and pet the dog.

"Brewer?" Bexley whispered.

When he stood and met her gaze, she charged toward him, slamming into the thick arms she'd dreamt about every night for the past four and a half months. After her gave her a powerful embrace that squeezed all air from her lungs, she pressed thankful kisses to every inch of his beautiful face before the glorious moment their mouths finally reconnected. Her heart swelled when he swept her off her feet and carried her toward their bedroom.

CHAPTER TWENTY

"I've waited one hundred and thirty two days for the moment I could lay in this bed with you like this again," Brewer said to Bexley, hooking his bare leg around hers and kissing her forehead. "Not that I counted or anything."

"Was it everything you hoped for?" she asked.

"Can't say I'm disappointed."

"Careful, or I'll start to think you're becoming both domesticated *and* romantic." She traced her finger over the battered flag on his shoulder down to the next set of tattoos on his bicep, amazed they hadn't stretched or become distorted with the growth of his muscles. "I should've guessed you'd want to surprise me, rather than telling me when I could expect you."

"I hated to get your hopes up when the prosecutor kept jerking us around."

"None of that matters anymore." She glanced up at him. "I'm so glad you're home, Hawk. While you were gone, I realized something important about myself."

He lifted one eyebrow. "That I'm *not* blowing smoke up your ass every time I've told you that you're gorgeous, and one of a kind?"

She swatted at his chest, laughing, then pressed her lips to the same spot. Then she met his gaze once again. "I realized that I don't need anyone in my life. I'm strong and independent, and can survive just about anything on my own."

"I've always known that—doesn't mean I like hearing you say it," he muttered. Frowning, his fingers ran through her hair before settling against her jaw. "Are you breaking up with me, Squires?"

"The exact opposite." Grinning, she placed her hand over his. "I *want* you in my life. More than anything. I couldn't stand not having the freedom to tell you how my day went, or ask your advice. Everything bad that happened while you were away made me feel even more empty. I wanted you there to comfort me, and tell me everything was going to be alright." Tears filled her eyes as she sat up and took his face in her hands. "I can't promise I'll ever want to have your children—for reasons that have nothing to do with you, but I can promise I'll never want you anywhere other than right here with me. In this house. For as long as we both shall live…or until you get tired of my antics and kick me out. Whichever comes first. Only if you want to, that is. If you're not into it, we can go another round until you forget I ever said anything."

A smile stretched over his kissable lips. "Are you, the unshakable Bexley Squires, saying what I think you're saying?"

"I want to marry you, Hawk."

With a grave expression, his Adam's apple bobbed as he swallowed and gave a single nod. "Then I guess there's only one thing I have to say to that." He suddenly moved out from beneath her, flipping her around to her back. He then bent to kiss her long and hard, stopping once they were both breathless. He leaned back with a dazzling smile. "*Hell yeah* I'll marry you!"

She felt her smile grow to match his. "Sorry I don't have a ring. I mean…this was so unexpected. I'll take you to the mall and let you pick one out. You'd look great in something sparkly. Maybe something with little pink stones on the sides."

Next thing she knew, he was tickling her until she was begging for mercy between breathless laughter. The dog came charging into the room, barking in their ears.

"Get 'im, Cap!" Bexley commanded. "Lick 'im to death, boy!"

Brewer hoisted the dog up onto the bed. The two of them engaged in a wiggling mess of weird noises/barks and wet kisses. "Mommy and daddy are getting married, Cap!" Brewer told him. "We're gonna be a real family!"

Bexley's heart was full.

Together, Twila and Temperance had turned Temperance's backyard into a floral wonderland of white. Chairs, linens, candles…even Cap and Cinderella had been made to wear white bandanas even though they'd been banished to the mansion for the day. Flowers of every shape and size climbed trellises as far as the eye could see. Rows of upscale folding chairs and white runners faced the grand arbor overlooking the ocean. It was enough to make Bexley feel ill as she stood behind the mansion, taking it all in.

"What is the matter, *mi amiga?*" Temperance asked, setting a hand on her cocked hip. "You do not like it?"

"It's a little…colorless." Bexley eyed her friend's intricate braids, and her elaborate satin dress the same dusty shade of pink as all the bridesmaids. She didn't want to know how much the dresses had cost. Kiersten had merely instructed everyone what they were wearing, and picked up the bill. "You, on the other hand, are stunning."

Temperance released her signature tinkling laugh. "Have you looked into a mirror today?"

"Don't change the subject. You're so beautiful that I expect any single men who see you are going to drop on their knees and beg for your hand in marriage, on the spot. We'll have to ask for the minister to stay and perform another ceremony."

Temperance threw her arm around Bexley's shoulder. "You always make me laugh, Miss Bexley! It's no wonder our Olive always begs me to visit you!"

"Where is that little ball of fire?" Bexley asked, scanning the sea of white.

"She is somewhere inside…maybe in her room. She wanted it extra clean in case someone wanted to come see it."

"I'll have to go give it a look," Bexley decided, patting her friend on the shoulder. "I'll catch up with you later, Temp. Don't go running off with any handsome suitors before the ceremony."

Hordes of caterers and waiters hustled about near the mansion, setting up fountains and table decorations for the reception. Bexley darted around them, intending to head inside, when she was hooked around the waist and dragged backward near a set of tall bushes. She didn't have time to yelp before Brewer's warm lips were on hers. Kissing with an audience was still a new novelty, but she'd learned to accept his affection in the several months since his release. Before too long, she was so into the kiss that she nearly forgot they weren't alone.

"Damn, you are the hottest woman I've ever laid eyes on," he muttered as they parted, his lips still lingering on hers. "Can you wear that dress every night?"

"Only if you'll wear *that suit* every moment for the rest of your life," she decided, pulling on the lapel. His hair, finally grown out to a longer length, was slicked back in a style she hadn't seen on him before, and his arms bulged inside the gray designer suit worn over a crisp white dress shirt. As attractive as he looked, she feared she'd spend the night challenging other women to a duel. "Even surfing."

Brewer kissed her again, then drew back with a smirk. "This wedding thing has gotten me in some kind of mood." He wiggled his eyebrows. "Wanna sneak off somewhere for a little while so I can see what you're wearing under that dress, my beautiful wife?"

Bexley clamped a hand over his mouth and desperately searched the area to see if anyone was listening. "Shhh…someone will hear you!"

Prying her fingers off his mouth, he chuckled. "I don't know why you insist on keeping the fact that we're married a secret, B."

"Because this is *Kiersten's* big day. I don't want to steal her spotlight."

"Except we've been married since *June*."

"I didn't want to diminish her excitement in any way. You know how she is…she would've insisted we throw a massive reception like this one, and that's just not how I roll. I picture us doing something much smaller and more intimate—kind of like our wedding." When she recalled their little barefoot ceremony behind their cottage on the beach, with only the justice of the peace present, she felt as if she was floating. They'd worn their outfits from New Year's Eve—her in the white pants suit Kiersten picked out for their reunion, Brewer in his navy blue suit. "I guarantee I won't let our reception look like the Stay Puft Marshmallow Man vomited all over the place."

"When are you going to start wearing your ring?"

"After Cin and Alex get married." She patted the spot it occupied between her cleavage, safely hidden on a long chain. "I don't want to take anything away from my sister, either."

His eyes flashed with hurt. "So I'll just keep being your dirty little secret?"

"Maybe I just want to keep this between us for now because it's so special, and I don't want to share it with anyone." She wrapped her arms around his thick waist and hummed with content. "I still can't believe I get to wake up next to you every morning, my sexy husband."

"Get used to it, B. I'm not going anywhere."

They started to kiss again when they were interrupted by a deep throat clearing. "Sorry," Grayson stammered. "I didn't—"

"No problem," Bexley insisted, giving Brewer a playful nudge away. She eyed her ex-boyfriend's suit the same style and cut as Brewer's. It fit much differently on someone who hadn't spent four months of their life obsessively doing push ups, but he was still handsome. "You look great, Gray."

"You do too," he replied. His eyes swung over to Brewer. "I've been meaning to apologize for what went down at the reunion. I was an ass to both of you. Guess I didn't adjust to things very well."

Brewer shrugged with a serious expression. "We all have our demons."

Grayson slipped both hands into his suit pants pockets and turned to Bexley. "I also wanted to tell you before you heard from someone else that I'm moving to Florida next week."

Lips dropping open, Bexley blanched. "What?"

"I'm transferring to a small island. It's laid back and void of any controversy or corruption." Shrugging his shoulders, he grinned. "It was time for a change."

Her heart sank. She'd enjoyed their renewed friendship over the past several months. "Does this have something to do with Sofia?"

"We stopped seeing each other early summer. A buddy I met in the academy offered me the position. He highly recommends the area—said it'll be less stress, fewer hours."

Closing the distance between them, Bexley

wrapped him in her arms with a profound sense of loss. "I'll miss you."

"At least I can rest easy knowing you're in good hands." He only hugged her back for a few seconds before releasing her.

"Brewer and I got married," she blurted, stepping back. "A couple of months ago."

A genuine smile spread over Grayson's lips when he offered Brewer his hand. "Congratulations. Take good care of her." Bexley thought she saw him wince with Brewer's grip.

"Bet your ass I will," her husband replied.

With their exchange, Bexley's sunken heart soared. They had never gotten together for dinner as she'd requested, but at least they could part ways on good terms.

"Guess I'll catch you later," Grayson told them with a dismissive tilt of his head.

"I better see you busting a move on the dance floor later!" Bexley called after him. He waved dismissively over his shoulder.

"Thought we weren't telling anyone," Brewer whispered, dragging her back into his arms.

"Thought I'd make an exception under the circumstances." She kissed him chastely before stepping backwards toward the house. "I'm heading up to see Olive's room. Save the first dance for me, handsome."

He winked. "You've permanently filled my dance card, Squires."

She giggled, knowing he'd always call her that even if she eventually decided to take his name. There was an added skip in her step as she entered Temperance's home. On her journey through the second story of the complex mansion, she spotted her neighbor adjusting her mentor's tie through the cracked door of a guest room.

"Hold still," Twila commanded. "I've never met such an ornery old coot in my life."

"I may be old, but I ain't ornery, darlin'," J.J. drawled. "You've merely forgotten what it's like to be with the masculine type rather than those hippies and European snobs you dated back in the day."

Bexley slapped her hand over her mouth before they heard her snort. She'd introduced them the night they'd thrown Brewer a welcome-home party. Based on their conversation, she assumed they'd kept in touch. *Close* touch.

"What are you doing?" Cineste asked, making her jump. "Kiersten is looking for you."

Bexley spun around to address her, deciding she

easily took the cake for the most beautiful bridesmaid with her growing baby bump, amped cleavage, and the glow of her rosy cheeks.

"How's she holding up?"

"She's being…Kiersten," Cineste decided with a roll of her eyes. "Come talk her down before she has a meltdown."

They passed several doors before arriving in Temperance's master suite. Bexley was immediately reminded of the reason Kiersten had agreed to Temperance's idea of having the wedding on her property after their original venue had double-booked and canceled their reservations. The rich mix of soft colors and textures draped from the high ceilings created a fairytale backdrop for the stunning bride. The simple ivory dress Kiersten wore was a lovely blend of lace over the fitted bodice, spilling down onto the tulle skirt. Kiersten's complicated hairstyle and flawless makeup courtesy of Temperance's professional team made her look as if she had stepped right out of a high-fashion bridal magazine. Her mother and aunt fussed with the skirt when Kiersten spun around to face Bexley, eyes wide.

"I don't have anything blue!" she exclaimed. "How the hell did I forget to plan for something blue? It's bad luck, Bex. The *worst*. I can't start a marriage out that way!"

"You didn't think your maid of honor would have it covered?" Bexley scoffed. Activating her quick wit, she removed the chain from around her neck and deposited the pale blue diamond ring fused with an antique silver band in the palm of her best friend's hand. "Voilà. Problem solved."

Kiersten let out a high-pitched noise. "What's this?" she demanded, thrusting her other hand in emphasis. "*What is this?*"

"Relax before you break something we can't afford to replace!" Bexley huffed. "I'll explain later. Just put the damn thing on your finger before you have a Bridezilla moment."

Cineste made an ear-shattering noise similar to Kiersten's. "Bex, is that—"

"I'm gonna check on Olive!" Bexley announced, dashing toward the hallway.

She slammed the door behind her a moment before her sister and best friend's voices exploded with excitement. *"Oh my god!" "I can't believe it!" "Do you think they really got married without telling us?"*

As she knocked on Olive's door across the hall-way, she was grateful she'd been spared the crushing hugs and sloppy kisses that would've undoubtedly followed.

"Come in!" Olive yelled.

Beneath a chandelier and billowing curtains draped over a four-poster bed, Olive sat in a pile of pillows with both dogs snuggled in on either side, reading. She'd become a bookworm in the past several months, with an overflowing bookshelf as proof. The room was feminine and elegant, with only a handful of stuffed animals to prove it belonged to a young girl.

"Your room is *awesome*," Bexley said, moving to sit beside her on the mattress. She'd never felt a comforter so soft and fluffy. "You've collected more books since I was last here."

Olive closed the book and looked up at Bexley. "Wow. I've never seen you look so pretty. Has Brewer seen you yet?"

"I think he liked the dress," Bexley said, nodding. "And you, Miss Thing, you could be mistaken for a *real* princess."

With a proud smile, Olive smoothed her hands over the dress. It was the same color as all the bridesmaids' with a higher neck and longer skirt. "I *feel* like a real princess. Temperance makes me feel that way all the time though. I told her she needs to knock it off so the social workers don't think she's *too* nice."

"I don't think there's such a thing in a social worker's eyes. Speaking of, it won't be long before the termination hearing. How are you feeling about that?"

"I wish it was sooner. They said Sadie won't be out of jail before I graduate from high school, and this is where I want to stay."

With a sudden rush of adoration for the young girl, Bexley took her hand. "I'm glad you came into our lives, Olive."

Olive launched herself into Bexley's arms. "Me too, Aunt Bexley." She squeezed Bexley a little tighter. "If I'm truly a princess now, that makes you my fairy godmother. Thanks to you, I get to live happily ever after."

Bexley laughed, squeezing the girl back. Everyone she loved had gotten their own version of a happily ever after.

ABOUT THE AUTHOR

With over 40 captivating titles spanning various genres, Quinn Avery honed her talent for crafting intricate puzzles through her smart and quirky Bexley Squires mystery series. Her contemporary suspense thrillers, often set in her beloved locales such as Lake Shetek and Mankato, Minnesota, are nothing short of addictive, leaving readers spellbound with their mind-spinning twists.

For more information, and a free ebook, visit www.QuinnAvery.com.

ACKNOWLEDGMENTS

I'd like to send a heartfelt thank you to the fans of this series for always wanting more Bexley! While this book was the end of her adventures *for now*, I'm open to the possibility of another book if the circumstances feel right. Although Grayson wasn't right for Bexley, I'm excited to announce his story will continue in my new Tiki Trouble cozy mystery series coming in 2021!

Bexley Squires wouldn't exist without the help from my awesome tribe that helps to make this series what it is. Huge thank you to Najla Qamber for the excellent cover, Jodi Henley for the stellar advice, Lisa Frommie for the jailhouse procedures, my mom and Jenny Hanson for proofreading, and my awesome son Owen for your feedback.

www.ingramcontent.com/pod-product-compliance
Lightning Source LLC
Chambersburg PA
CBHW011414310726
48972CB00011B/2978